For *Jim and Anne* . . . . . for always being there

With all my love

THE RIDDLE OF KEBOR'S MESA

ANNE B. CIOTTI

Copyright - March 2013
Mindset Publications
anneciotti@gmail.com

Cover Image by Anne B. Ciotti

and

Durra-Quick Print Inc.

ISBN: 978-0-9890794-0-2

FORWARD

Most of the cities and towns in this work of fiction were made up by the author. All of the people and the events that took place are pure fiction. Any resemblance to persons living or dead is coincidental.

This story is about Paul Briarwood, a man whose heart is tuned to the drumbeat of his Mowkatah Indian heritage; and to his son Billy who, marching to the beat of his own heart, answers to the call of Kebor's Mesa and finds intrigue and a trip to the stars and beyond. The novel is whimsical. It is laced with romance, mystery, and spirituality. It was written for the reading pleasure of the young and the young at heart.

Anne B. Ciotti

ACKNOWLEDGEMENTS

To Jim and Anne, my beloved son and daughter-in-law, thank you for maintaining a warm and harmonious atmosphere in our home. Without it there would be little creative effort on my part. And for never saying it couldn't be done.

To Gayle Swedmark Hughes who gave unselfishly and asked for nothing in return; thank you Gayle for your encouragement and guidance every step of the way.

Thank you, Dr. Pamela Kennedy for taking time out from a busy schedule to edit this work of fiction. Your suggestions have greatly enhanced the quality of my work.

Last but not least, a big thanks to the many friends who cheered me on and inspired me from the side lines.

Anne B. Ciotti

TABLE OF CONTENTS

Dedication
Forward
Acknowledgements

		Page
Prologue		1
Ch I	Paul Briarwood	7
Ch II	Redbud, North Carolina	17
Ch III	The Hollisters	28
Ch IV	Paul, the Civilian	36
Ch V	The Honeymoon	61
Ch VI	David and Michael	68
Ch VII	Sarah's Demise	79
Ch VIII	Kathy and Paul Move to Redbud	88
Ch IX	Restoration of the Hollister House	98
Ch X	Kathy and Peggy Commiserate	105
Ch XI	Billy is Born	111

Table of Contents Continued

		Page
Ch XII	Billy in the First Person	115
Ch XIII	Billy, a Seeker of Truth	121
Ch XIV	David Turns Fourteen	132
Ch XV	Billy Climbs Kebor's Mesa	139
Ch XVI	Billy's Ninth Birthday	150
Ch XVII	Baseball and the Duggan's	163
Ch XVIII	Organized Baseball	170
Ch XIX	Beginning of a Tough Year	177
Ch XX	Billing Goes Hunting	198
Ch XXI	Mishap at Duggan's	209
CH XXII	Kebor's Mesa Calls	217
Ch XXIII	Elyce	226
Ch XXIV	Elyce's Philosophy	251
Ch XXV	Back to Earth	267
Ch XXVI	Epilogue	273

PROLOGUE

There I sat in my favorite spot, eight hundred feet or so above the valley floor, gazing out at the Great Smokey Mountains. With my hands locked around my knees and my knees pulled up to my chin, I tried to make sense of the day's events. At fourteen years of age, I was bankrupt; a hopeless speck of humanity perched on the brink of the world, searching in vain for a way out of my troubles.

A myriad of stars shone brightly in a cloudless sky. Cascading waters, a string of lakes, and the Little Limerick River below, reflected silver in the light of a pale moon. Ebony silhouettes defined the rounded peaks of Mount Angel Head, Les Capitan's Fortress, and Mount Rhoda. Save for the din of night creatures and the language of the wind in the trees, all was still.

As always, I sensed the power in the vast expanse; it held me spellbound and made me feel infinitesimally small and trivial. At the same time it calmed me and helped me think more clearly.

Time and time again my thoughts went through the day's events from the morning's hunt to the mishap on the Campbell farm. The sight of the Campbell's prize cow Bessie lying dead in the barn was never out of mind. Something was oddly out of focus with the picture I projected; but for the life of me, I couldn't put a finger on it.

I pondered my predicament until my head throbbed and I could no longer think coherently. The chill in the air began to penetrate my clothing. Sternly, I told myself that I should return home before my absence was discovered. Still, I lingered; my mind on my problems and my eyes on the stars glittering overhead, appearing like thousands of diamonds in a blue-black vault.

Suddenly, one of the points of light broke away from its fixed position in the sky and began to behave erratically. Bewildered, I unfolded my legs, leaned forward, and squinted. I thought it was a star and cupped a hand to my forehead to study the phenomenon more intently. No, it was not a star, I reasoned; stars do not do loops. Then what could it be? Was it a daredevil pilot testing a highly maneuverable military plane under the cover of night? Or, perhaps it was a mad scientist who was also sitting under these same stars playing with his latest toy by remote control.

Finally, I realized that the craft, whatever it might be, was in serious trouble. Fascinated, I watched it shorten the distance between us. As it drew closer it abruptly stopped, swerved and shot upward. Just when I thought it was going to disappear from sight, it began to spiral downward again. At that point, the unbelievable happened; an entity, speaking in a foreign language, contacted me telepathically.

"Please help me," was the message it conveyed.

Strange, to *hear* a string of weird syllables in your head without the benefit of sound; and even stranger, to have them translated automatically into a recognizable thought, as if by magic. And, as if by magic, I knew at once that the entity was of female gender.

I had tickled the underbelly of mental telepathy on several occasions, but my capabilities were limited. For me it either happened or it didn't; it wasn't something I could control or call up at will. Even so, every fiber of my being prompted me to respond to the distress plea, as strange as it was.

Doing as Dad had instructed me, I closed my eyes and concentrated hard on the alien being I now envisioned, trying to transmit my own thoughts into the ether.

"I'm Billy Briarwood. Are you real, or am I stuck in a dream? Besides, how could I possible help you? You're up there, I'm down here, and levitation is not one of my strong suits."

"I will show you the way, Billy," the alien responded eagerly.

Ceasing to spiral, the object now hurtled straight toward earth at a tremendously fast rate of speed. I held my breath. In seemingly no lapse of time it made a ninety-degree turn, slid sideways across the horizon, and stopped to hover over Mount Angel Head. It continued to hover there for a fraction of a second before plunging into the trees and tumbling end over end down the mountainside.

In a blinding flash of light the show was over. From what I could tell, the object had crashed somewhere on the far side of the river, almost in a direct line with my position on Kebor's Mesa. I watched for any sign of a fire that may have resulted from the accident, but none ever materialized.

Minutes of eerie silence passed as I waited for further contact; then....

"Help me, please."

"I would like to help you, but I don't know how. You see, I'm in trouble up to my armpits right now. I should be home in bed."

"Where is home?"

"I live in the Hollister house in the valley on the other side of this mesa," I said, pointing.

"Hmm, Billy Briarwood lives in the Hollister House. Interesting." Although the alien's musings were not intended for me to *hear,* somehow I picked up on them. "And *house* is *home*? Two words for one thing?"

"Well, yes, I guess so," I answered.

"You can help me, Billy. You have exactly what I need in your pants pouch."

"Do you mean my pants pocket?"

"Yes, in your pocket. Help me and I promise to find a way to help you," the voice pleaded.

"Humph!" I snorted, "I'll help you if I can, but I doubt if you can do anything to help me; you don't know my father."

"Who is your father?" the entity asked.

"Paul…. Paul Briarwood."

The Riddle of KEBOR's MESA

Chapter I

Paul Briarwood

Paul Briarwood was born on February 17, 1925 to a French-Canadian and Irish mother, and a French-Canadian and Mowkatah Indian father in Britt's Bay City, North Carolina. The Indian blood coursing through Paul's veins fueled his love of nature and demanded that he fish and hunt. Under his father's tutelage, he learned to cane-pole fish for crappie before he cut his eye teeth. According Mowkatah Indian tradition he went "on-the-hunt" at the age of fourteen as a rite of passage into manhood.

On his initial hunting expedition he brought down an antlered buck with a single shot fired from a Winchester rifle at ninety yards. The trophy kill confirmed his standing as a man among men within the broad circle of his native relatives and, furthermore, established him as a true marksman.

Within a week of graduating from high school in June of 1942, he went to work as an apprentice carpenter for Avery Pomeroy, the city's principal building contractor.

Although he was only seventeen years of age, he had developed into a serious minded youth possessing uncanny instincts and high moral standards. A model of masculinity, Paul stood five-feet, eleven-inches. He had broad shoulders and slim hips. Raven-black hair formed a mass of unruly curls on his head and around the nape of his neck. His dark gray eyes were flecked with silver and almost always carried the hint of a twinkle. As though the whole world amused him, his laughter flowed as freely as honey on a warm day. Seldom did he display anger, but when he did you saw the dark, unreadable side of him. Grim faced, his eyes would turn as hard as flint and bore into your very soul. Fortunately, the moment of anger was usually short lived.

Paul's association with Avery Pomeroy, comfortable from the outset, quickly turned into a close friendship. Unexpectedly, carpentry gave Paul a great deal of personal satisfaction. He liked the smell of wood, the feel of it, the beauty in its grains, and its unique properties. He decided to make carpentry his life's work. Someday he, Paul Briarwood, would make a name for himself designing and building custom homes.

Ah, yes, someday....., someday....., after he had had fulfilled his obligation to Uncle Sam and the war to end all wars was over.

On February 17, 1943, Paul celebrated his eighteenth birthday; on the same day he joined the United States Army. For more than two and a half years, he served with a support unit in the European Theater of Operations, answering to an Army Officer's commands.

Serving in the eye of the storm, he had his fill of the action and he earned his share of the medals. Although risk-taking always figured into the equation when dealing with the enemy, his acute senses, instincts, and a good measure of luck, leveled the playing field.

In the middle of 1945, atomic bombs exploded on the cities of Hiroshima and Nagasaki in Japan, sending shock waves around the globe. As a consequence, World War II came to an abrupt end on September 2, 1945. Paul had survived the war unscathed.

On Tuesday, October 2, 1945, he bid farewell to his good buddies and boarded a crowded troop carrier bound for an Army Air Force Base in Maryland. The next day he flew commercial to Ashville, North Carolina. A taxi took him from the airport to the train station where he bought a one-way ticket to Britt's Bay.

Now, reclining in a window seat on an eastbound train, he looked out at the pristine beauty of the Great Smokey Mountains, painted in an array of autumn colors. Lazily, he let his mind drift. In retrospect, he realized that the war had taken him to the brink of hell and back again; but then, if it had not been for the war, he may never have formed a relationship with Kathleen Hollister.

Kathleen Hollister lived in the small valley town of Redbud where her formal education ended with the eighth grade. To continue her schooling she was obliged to catch an early morning bus to Britt's Bay to attend high school there. A grade behind Paul, Kathleen's path crossed his when their two classes were involved in the same social function. In the course of time they had become acquainted and, in fact, had dated several times, but had never connected romantically. After he left home to join the Army and had served for almost a year, he received a letter from her asking if he would like to be her pen-pal. The request came as a surprise.

The four-by-six inch snapshot she had enclosed with her letter showed a teenage girl with long chestnut colored hair pulled up in a ponytail. Incredibly blue eyes, the shade of cornflowers, gazed directly into his from the photo. Fringed with long dark lashes, those blue eyes were warm and lively. A pleasing smile displayed a dimple in her left cheek and perfect white teeth. She appeared tall and lithe – almost boyish - but ample curves in all the right places left no doubt as to her femininity. He had recalled a girl slightly shorter and pencil thin.

Her first letter to him had been rather generic, but interesting enough to pique his curiosity. Although he had been extremely tired, he had felt compelled to answer her letter that very evening.

Starting cautiously, the pen-pal relationship gradually developed into a trusting friendship. Soon, they began to confide intimate details about themselves; their likes and dislikes, their hopes and dreams.

Via airmail, they bonded. Eventually, they revealed their mutual feelings of love; but both sensibly acknowledged the fact that until they could meet once again in person, their true sentiments could not be known for certain. They both accepted the possibility that everything they perceived to be endearing might prove to be delusional or misunderstood on either or both their parts. Now, the answer was in the offing.

For want of sleep, Paul drew the shade on the window and closed his eyes. With his vision shut down, his sense of hearing became acute and creative. As he listened to the pounding rhythm of the train's wheels on the track, he found that he could transform the "clickity-clack" into any word or phrase he imagined. "The war is over, the war is over, the war is over," the song of the wheels reminded him for miles on end. For another long stretch of track the wheels repeated his pen-pal's name again and again – "Kathleen Hollister, Kathleen Hollister, Kathy, Kathy, Kathy." Finally, he tuned into the sound that eased his wanting soul, "I'm going home, I'm going home, home, home, home…." The words echoed relentlessly until they lulled him into a deep, drug-induced like sleep.

Upon reaching Britt's Bay, the train's wailing whistle and the hush of the engine braking to a halt woke him with a start. Straightening in his seat, he rubbed his eyes and ran his fingers over short-cropped hair; then he rose and smoothed the wrinkles from his uniform. Picking up his duffle bag, he stepped from the train onto the platform of the terminal. For a tense moment he stood quietly; wary steel gray eyes searching for a familiar face in a sea of strangers.

Meanwhile, his father was craning his neck from side to side, trying to see around the people blocking his passage. He had noted the lone soldier the moment he detrained and had wondered if he could possibly be the same boy who had left home so many months ago to serve his country. Then he caught a glimpse of the straight nosed profile and knew his beloved son was back where he belonged. His heartbeat quickened and he advanced toward the man in long quick strides, shouting, "Paul, Paul."

Wrinkles, deeper than Paul remembered, etched his father's tan skin; skin made leathery from years spent working as a surveyor for the Army Corps of Engineers. Mark Briarwood, Sr. had shrunken a bit, but even so, he was still an imposing figure; still considerably tall and arrow straight in gray serge pants and a hand-knit white

The Riddle of Kebor's Mesa

sweater. Paul would have been disappointed if the elder man had not been wearing a blue shirt; his favorite color for happy occasions.

"Welcome home," his father exclaimed and, making an effort to hold his emotions in check, gathered his son in a rib-crushing embrace. "We have missed you, my son," he whispered against Paul's cheek. "Your mother and I have been worried out of our minds."

Standing back, he assessed the returning soldier anxiously. "You're taller Paul and you've muscled out….," he said and hesitated. "As a matter of fact you look downright fine, but….? Oh shit, Paul, just tell me, how much damage did they do to you? Are you all right? Are you really all right?"

"My Guardian Angel worked overtime, Dad; there's nothing wrong with me that time won't heal. However, I am tired and hungry."

Dangling a set of car keys in front of his son, the older man asked, "Are you up to driving?"

Paul grinned and nodded. "Just lead me to the old Buick."

"How about driving that old 1939 Chevy sedan you see parked at the curb? You might want to be careful with it though, it belongs to you," his father exclaimed. "It was a wreck before your brother got his hands on it. He overhauled it and fine-tuned it. Between us we managed to scrounge enough gas to fill the tank. Now let's get going; your mother has prepared food that would please royalty. And a crowd of people are waiting to welcome home my favorite son."

"I thought Mark was your favorite son," Paul retorted.

After witnessing the birth of four daughters before having a son, Paul's father named the boy after himself, but refused to call him Junior. The baby became "Mark," and he became "Senior" to those who knew him well.

"Mark is favorite son number one and you are favorite son number two."

Chapter II

REDBUD, N.C.

As Paul and his father closed in on 1427 Randolph Street the sun was painting streaks of gold and copper in a twilight sky. Home had never looked more inviting. A large "Welcome Home" banner was stretched above the entrance of the house. Red, white, and blue balloons wafted in the breeze from strings tethered to shrubbery.

Leaving the doorway jammed with gawking people, Clara Briarwood dashed down the front steps to greet her returning son with outstretched arms. "Paul, oh Paul," she cried.

Unmindful of his tears, Paul wrapped his arms around his mother and, with his cheek in her hair, held her long and lovingly. Then he wiped the tears from her eyes and studied her intently.

She, too, had aged during his absence. The brown in her hair was yielding to silver, and she had resorted to wearing flat heeled shoes as opposed to the two-inch heels she was in the habit of wearing when he left. However, a beaded headband, her trademark, held her hair in place, as always. Some things never change, he thought – thank God.

Feeling a rush of adrenalin, Paul forgot that he was exhausted and starved; Clara, however, did not. Taking his hand, she gently pulled him indoors where people waited and an abundance of scrumptious food was ready to be served.

Paul, the man of the hour, partook of the food with a ravenous appetite, leaving only enough room for a final cup of coffee and a slice of German chocolate cake.

For several hours, in an atmosphere filled with positive energy, he reconnected with the people closest to his heart – his brother and sisters and their families; his uncles, aunts, and cousins; his friends and neighbors. When it was over and the guests had departed, he bid his parents, "Goodnight," and went upstairs to his room; happy to find everything as it had been before he left for boot camp. He showered and crawled into his very own bed, thinking of Kathy. Tomorrow, after breakfast, he would call her and arrange for a Saturday date. They would go dining and dancing; they would hold hands and talk into the wee hours of the morning about – what else? – possibilities.

That Saturday, he groomed himself with extra care, pinning his ribbons and service medals to the chest of a crisp, fresh Army jacket, hoping to impress Kathy and her parents. Next week he would be wearing civilian clothing and his uniform would be stored in mothballs.

Departing from home well ahead of schedule, he again thanked his parents for the car, settled in the driver's seat, and headed for Redbud.

At the intersection of Randolph Street and Academy Boulevard - a four lane thoroughfare also known as State Route 462 - he stopped to let a string of westbound vehicles pass, then made a left turn and merged with eastbound traffic, speeding to get around a slow-moving car to position himself in the right turn lane.

Immediately past the turnoff for the Blue Ridge Parkway, he impulsively drove onto an exit ramp that took him on a country road known to shorten the distance to Redbud by several miles. The road twisted and turned with the lay of the land over a series of low-lying hills. He recalled it as being passable. Now it was filled with ruts and rocks and potholes that yawed wide and deep. He cursed the time he lost getting to County Road 97; the two lane macadam highway that connected Redbud with mainstream America. Changes, subtle and not so subtle, were everywhere. He felt like a stranger in the land of his birth.

At the approach of the small town, he drove onto the shoulder of the road on top of a hill, stopped the car and got out. From his vantage point he could see the entire valley. He filled his lungs and wondered if this was where destiny awaited him.

Nestled in the foothills of the mountains, Redbud was shaped like a shallow bowl canted toward the south. It was typical of small towns everywhere, featuring a Town Hall built of red-brick with mylar trim and an impressive clock tower. The edifice sat in the center of the town square which, in turn, was surrounded by a variety of businesses. A large number of modest, similar looking houses lined a grid of streets within the town proper. A dozen or so century old homesteads lined the north side of the highway, posing sedately on manicured lawns beneath the shade of mighty oaks and white pine trees. In sharp contrast, a scattering of mobile homes and summer cottages sat in selective spots in a grove of sheltering trees on the south side of the road.

He took in the large three-story, box-like building in the center of town and decided that it was the school. And the big, gray rectangular building squatting next to two grain elevators near the highway on the east end had to be the Fulton Lumber & Grain Co. The skeletal framework of the water tower and the little white church sitting high on a grassy knoll replicated scenes also common in small towns.

The environs made the difference. It was the beauty of the environs in which the town nestled that greatly enhanced its charm.

Great forests blanketed the hilltops in all directions. To the south, hundreds of acres of cultivated fields could be seen, some of which bore the stubble left from a recent harvest. Beyond the fields in the near distance, half hidden in terrain gone wild, two elongated amoeba-shaped lakes mirrored the cloudy sky.

Above the town looking north, Black Angus cattle and sorrel horses grazed in green pastures. They slaked their thirst on the waters of a swift, narrow river that poured through a gap in the base of Rocky Ridge just east of Kebor's Mesa.

Rocky Ridge, reaching no more than a hundred feet in height at any one spot, stretched east and west as far as Paul could see; here and there piles of scree crumbled from its sides. The jagged wall separated the foothills to the south from the mountains to the north. However, the highest mountains in the area were blocked from view by the monumental mesa-like formation that rose from the spine of the ridge. Theoretically, mesas do not exist in North Carolina; however, Kebor's Mesa was a fair name for the formation named after the man who first noticed its peculiarity at the turn of the nineteenth century.

Paul had seen the mesa before, but only in passing. On that day it captured his interest; probably because Kathy had mentioned it in her letters. She had begun to climb to the top of the formation at the age of nine, she told him. To aid the war effort during the war she had sat on top of the mesa and searched the sky for enemy planes.

For several minutes more, he puzzled over the unexplainable marvel and wondered how many people observed it every day without even a glimmer of really seeing its uniqueness. But then, did it really matter?

Chimes on the clock tower announced the half hour – 3:30 PM. With a half hour to spare, he went back to the car and hit the road again. Since there was no traffic behind him, he slowed down to read the two signs posted on an old plank bridge: The top one read: "Limerick River," and the one below: "Redbud – Population 1,483. On the far side of the bridge the road widened and a third sign read: "Main Street."

On the eastern perimeter of Redbud, Paul turned left onto East River Road, and followed it to the junction where East and North River Roads joined. He parked the car on the far side of a graveyard and walked back to the little white church. He paused to read yet another sign: 'St. Bartholomew's Presbyterian Church – Sunday Services – 8:15 and 11:00 AM."

Upon entering the empty church he sat in the very rear pew where he was least apt to be noticed and could easily depart without drawing attention to himself should the need arise. Committing himself to meditation, he mentally set a time limit, programming himself to awaken in fifteen minutes. Knowing that nagging thoughts and other unsettling conditions could keep him from reaching his goal, he made an effort to calm himself and then willed his mind to go completely blank. Within a matter of seconds, he became oblivious to his surroundings.

A quarter of an hour later he regained his conscious state of being. True to what he had come to expect, he experienced a spiritual vigor that had been lacking before the exercise. Satisfied, he rose to leave the pew only to find a blacked-robed figure sitting beside him.

Tall, rotund, balding, and wearing glasses, the reverend regarded him with a jovial kind of concern – anxious and amused at the same time. "Are you all right?" he asked. "You went deep, soldier. I've been sitting here for ten minutes and you didn't move a muscle."

"I use meditation as an elixir. It seldom fails me," Paul explained.

"Yes, it can be very beneficial, particularly if your attitude is right." The man tugged at the pointy brown beard on his chin and considered Paul candidly. "Is there anything I can do for you?"

"No, I'm fine, but thank you, Reverend. I'm on the way to see my girl. I had a few spare minutes, so…."

"But…., you appear to be empty handed," the reverend observed, giving Paul a side glance. "Oh, of course, the gift is in your car."

"Well, as a matter of fact I do have a box of chocolates - which isn't much. You see, I just got home a few days ago and I haven't had time to do anything but visit with my family."

"Then I can help you; come with me," the reverend said and scurried down the aisle toward the altar with Paul on his heels. "There was a wedding here this morning," he said. "The flowers on display have served their purpose; make a bouquet from the freshest of them while I find something to wrap them in." He then fled to the chamber behind the altar and came back a minute later waving a sheet of cellophane. This should do it," he exclaimed exuberantly.

"Thank you very much, Reverend. May I pay you for the flowers?"

"I should say not; I'm glad they were available."

"I'm Paul Briarwood, and your name is....?" Paul asked, offering his hand.

"Reverend Aloysius P. Burkham, or just plain Aloysius if you prefer," the man of cloth answered, gripping Paul's hand warmly. "Will I see you again, Paul?"

"I live in Britt's Bay, but I'll probably be visiting Redbud on weekends; so yes, I'm sure we'll meet again."

Chapter III

The Hollisters

The Hollister House was built on a five-acre parcel of land in the Nineteenth Century by Joseph Hollister's great grandfather Lucifer Hollister. The two-story house spoke of gracious living, refinement, and of days gone by. Situated well back from the road midst a host of stately trees, it featured handsome fireplace chimneys, a spindle-railed, wrap-around porch, and mullioned windows with workable shutters. The large attic above the living space had dormer windows on all four sides. A gravel driveway along the south side of the homestead led to a three-stall carriage house in the rear. Beyond the carriage house, a slatted wood fence encircled a small orchard containing apple and peach trees.

Paul parked in front of the residence and got out of the car carrying the candy and flowers. He was apprehensive and hesitant, wondering how he would be received. Well, now is not the time for timidity, he thought and, inhaling deeply, started across the lawn. Simultaneously, the front door swung open and the girl whose picture he had been carrying in his shirt pocket for ever so long appeared. A vision in a little black evening dress, flashing a dimpled smile, Kathleen Hollister came running down the steps to greet him. Then, suddenly shy and uncertain, she stopped her advance just out of arms reach.

Their eyes met and locked. As if their paths had come full circle, a fleeting flash of recognition passed between them. Paul stood as still as a statue, frozen in place, unable to respond to the natural order of things. His whole being tingled with the electricity that flowed between them, but still he could not move, nor could he force himself to look away.

It was Kathleen who stepped forward to draw nearer to him. Robot-like, Paul dropped the candy and flowers to the ground and swept her into his arms simply because it was impossible not to. "Oh Kathy, I've waited so long for this…. "

"Paul, Paul, you're here at last," she uttered huskily and, emitting a low whimper, put her arms around his neck and returned his passionate kiss.

Shuffling her feet to get their attention, Kathy's mother Sarah came and stood close by, making sure she placed herself where Paul could see her clearly.

Paul was aware of the pleasantly plump woman dressed in green. In a glance, he noticed her fiery red hair and cheerful face set with impish green eyes. Through lowered lids he dispatched a blink her way and then disregarded her. In his present state of bliss he could no more relinquish his hold on Kathy than he could fly without wings.

Then Sarah, in a harsh, throaty voice spoke, "Kathy, release him, it's my turn."

The sharp command, though said with humor, was sufficient to break the spell. The young couple separated.

The Riddle of Kebor's Mesa

Presenting the roses to Kathy, Paul said, "To you, with love." Then bowing from the waist, he offered the chocolates to Sarah. "These are for the lady to whom I will be eternally grateful for having given the world such a lovely daughter."

"Thank you handsome warrior, but forget the candy, I want a hug," she said and laughed. "Welcome home, soldier, from the bottom of my heart."

Any further dialog was squelched by the appearance of Joseph Hollister, Kathy's father. Tall, portly, and distinguished with a thick mass of graying hair, the President of the Mercantile Bank & Trust Co., in Britt's Bay, joined them; his hand extended. "Come inside where we can visit," he said.

"Yes," Sarah responded quickly, "go put the flowers in a vase Kathy. And Joseph, why don't you go and get a bottle of bubbly from the cellar so we can toast Paul's homecoming."

Moving rapidly, Paul followed Sarah's lead through the foyer and dining room to a sofa in the living room. On the way he could not help but gawk at the rich antique furnishings in the rooms. He was especially drawn to the elaborate crystal chandelier hanging above the dining room table.

"Your chandelier is difficult to pass by," he observed. The design is exquisite and the crystal is superb. It begs attention."

"It's a glorified dust catcher; nothing more," Sarah remarked, and sat opposite him in an overstuffed chair looking relaxed and smiling as though she were enjoying one of her own secret jokes. Casually, she proceeded to put a small flame to a cigarette, inhale the smoke deeply, and then blow the smoke out of the side of her mouth.

"I'm warning you, Paul Briarwood, harm a hair on my daughter's head and I will personally rip you apart." She made the statement with a flirtatious look, implying that she was jesting. Paul took her seriously.

"I would never do anything to hurt Kathy," he assured her.

"Fine, then that's settled, I've done my motherly duty. Now, suppose you tell me a little about yourself, Paul."

"There isn't much to tell," he began. "I was seventeen when I graduated from high school and went to work for Avery Pomeroy as an apprentice carpenter. When I turned eighteen I left the job to enlist in the Army. Thirty-two months later, I mustered out of the service with an honorable discharge and the rank of corporal. Someday, I want to design and construct custom homes. That's about it in a nutshell."

"When Joseph isn't involved with banking matters, he dabbles in furniture making. His work shop is in the carriage house; I'm sure he'd be happy to show it to you if you're interested."

"Another time perhaps, but not tonight; tonight belongs to Kathy and me," Paul said, looking up as Kathy entered the room and came to settle on the sofa beside him.

Sarah leaned back in her chair, took several puffs on the cigarette, then snuffed it out in an ashtray as her eyes traveled from Paul to Kathy and back again to Paul. They were engrossed in each other; holding hands, shoulders touching, apparently radiant with happiness. Was this for real? Or, was he merely using her daughter?

"I understand you are planning to take Kathy to Britt's Bay for dinner this evening." she said.

"That is the plan, Mrs. Hollister," Paul said.

"Oh, please, you've been knocking my daughter's socks off with your letters; call me Sarah. Would you consider having dinner with Joseph and me? It would save you some gas."

The unexpected offer had its merits. Paul turned to Kathy. "I've been planning this evening for a long time and I did promise to take you dancing," he said to her. "How do you feel about this?"

"I wouldn't mind staying here; we could play music and dance in the parlor later," Kathy answered, "I'll leave the decision up to you."

"Well, since gas rationing is a factor these days, and the aroma coming from the kitchen is quite appetizing, I'll agree to stay; but only if you have some waltz recordings in your collection."

Chapter IV

PAUL THE CIVILIAN

Ready or not, the days flew by in a rush. Paul crammed each one to the fullest, doing the things necessary for a smooth transition back into civilian life. The first thing he did was purchase a new wardrobe. Then, figuring that the burden of his keep should no longer fall on his parents shoulders - especially since his father was planning to retire soon - he found a furnished apartment and moved out of the family home. Next, he re-established his employment status with Avery Pomeroy and went back work full time.

He visited Kathy as often as possible, but no matter what else went on, he made it a point to be with her on Saturdays. On occasion, it was necessary to limit their activities to the Redbud area because of the gasoline shortage. At times, Paul brought his bicycle along to add to their options of things to do without having to rely on a motor vehicle.

One day they were bicycling just west of town with no particular goal in mind when they came upon a newly posted "For Sale" sign on a two-hundred acre parcel of land.

The sign excited Paul. Together he and Kathy toured the rippling terrain on their bicycles. Using natural trails, they rode from the ridge to the highway and back again, discovering bit by bit the unspoiled beauty of the property; the light forestry, the flowering shrubbery, and the sun spattering gold through the canopy of branches.

The property grabbed Paul's imagination. He envisioned it with home sites set among the trees and knew it had the potential for fulfilling his dream. A craving to own the property drew saliva; but at the same time he doubted that it was obtainable with his meager savings.

As much as he wanted to share his thoughts on the matter with Kathy, he refrained from doing so for fear of building hopes that would only falter and die. However, nothing would keep him from exploring his chances.

At the crack of dawn on a Saturday morning in November, he got out of bed with one thought in mind - either keep his *someday* dream on hold or put it in motion. To prepare himself, he went down on his knees, bowed his head reverently and, for the next half hour gave himself to his personal God in meditation. When he came out of the trance-like state he was ready to accept whatever fate sent him.

A cool revitalizing shower cleared his head further and enabled him to focus objectively. His mind was set. He was willing to spend every penny he had to own that two-hundred acre parcel and, if necessary, ask his father to lend him the money he lacked; in which case, of course, he would need Senior's approval.

Knowing that his parents never locked their doors, he entered their home on Randolph Street to find it filled with the tantalizing aroma of fresh-brewed coffee. At that early hour on a Saturday, it had to be his father who was up and about, not his mother.

After helping himself to a cup of the hot liquid eye-opener, he went to find his father at his work station in the rear of the laundry room, poring over a ledger; his pen poised to make an entry.

Seeing Paul put a frown on Senior's face. He set the pen aside and shifted his attention to his son.

"It's not much of an office; however, I find that I can think as clearly in small spaces as I can in big ones. Now, why don't you pull up a stool and talk to me; I can see that something is rattling around that head of yours."

"Well, yes, there is something on my mind," Paul responded, marveling at his father's ability to read him so readily. "I'd like you to take a ride with me to Clarksdale. The John Logan Real Estate Agency there has the listing for a parcel of land in the Redbud area that I am seriously thinking of buying."

"Sure, son, I'll go with you," his father said, then resumed working on the ledger that lay open on his desk. "I guess old habits do die hard. I am about to retire and here I am still recording every wrinkle, trickle, and rock slide I happen upon. Just give me a minute; a few more entries and I'll be done with this. Incidentally, I'd like to have a little breakfast before we go, okay?" he added, showing his unwillingness to be hurried.

"That's fine with me," Paul agreed, relaxing his posture and gulping a mouthful of coffee. "By the way, Dad, I want to bring Kathy here next week so you can meet her."

Minutes ticked by, during which time Senior neither said nor did anything but pose with a hand on his chin, deep in thought. Finally, he put the pen in his pocket, and closed the ledger. Then absently, he tamped tobacco into the bowl of a clay pipe he kept handy, placed the pipe between his teeth. After making sure the draft was right, he struck a match to the sole of his shoe and put the resulting flame to the pipe bowl. At once, the aroma of burning tobacco and wisps of swirling smoke arose to fill the air.

Not until then did Senior speak. "I hear your mother stirring in the kitchen so we have a few minutes," he began cautiously, swiveling his chair around to meet Paul's mystified look. "We'd love to meet your Kathy; any girl who can keep you away from Sunday dinner with the family must be special. However, I feel that you are moving too fast, Paul."

Put on the defensive, Paul felt the hair on the back of his neck stand up. "Why should I waste time? I'm in love with Kathy; I want to ask her to marry me," he stated firmly.

"You are in too much of a hurry for things. You are literally tripping over your own two feet to meet the deadlines you are setting for yourself. You couldn't wait to find an apartment so you could move out of your family home. You were barely settled when you went back to work."

"I know what I want, why not go after it?"

"You believe you know what you want; however, your views will change once you've recovered from the effects of the war."

Meeting his father's steely gaze, Paul refuted his father's statement. "There's little to recover from. It isn't as though I engaged in hand-to-hand combat or served in the trenches. Yes, I took chances and faced danger, but I survived. There isn't a scar on me," he retorted, even as he shivered involuntarily at the recollections of some of the horrors he had witnessed.

"Many of our deepest scars are the internal ones," Senior offered reflectively.

"You've made a good point, Dad. I admit that I saw more than I want to remember, but I'll get over it. As many men have said before me, it's death that draws the final curtain."

"The war has changed you, Paul," Senior pursued.

"I was a teenager when I left home so, of course, I've changed; I'm more experienced now."

"You should be taking life easy; lying in the sun; fishing, hunting. What happened to the man who loved to hunt? We're in the middle of the hunting season and you've made no mention of going hunting, not one time. See what I'm saying? The war robbed you of your love to hunt. That's what men do, they hunt and fish to put food on the table and to help maintain a balanced population in the animal kingdom. Using a gun to hunt for game has nothing to do with using a gun to kill another human. As I recall, you became a marksman at the age of fourteen; you upheld our tradition and you made me proud."

Mutely, Paul digested his father's criticism. It was true, he didn't care if he never saw a gun again, let alone fire one.

In a softer, more placating tone, Senior went on. "The life we build for ourselves should be filled with contentment and serenity. Sometimes it is better to sit back and let things develop on their own volition. It's all right to push, but not too hard. Going on the hunt used to make your face light up; you did the jig and showed such enthusiasm it made the cost well worth the effort. I would like to see you reclaim your love for the sport the war took away. Maybe not this year, but next year, say you'll go hunting with your brother and me."

The subject of Paul's failings was left at that. Senior was content in believing that he had given his son something to think about.

Actually, Senior had done more than give Paul something to think about. His chiding had put a damper on a day that had begun with high hopes. Was the chiding a precursor of things to come? an omen? Would the trip to Clarksdale prove futile? Should he even bother to go?

Clarksdale, a bustling city housing 67,000 people, was located about twenty miles north of Britt's Bay. John Logan's Real Estate Office was a straight shot up on the right side of State Route 462. Traffic was light. Paul and Senior were inside the door of the business exactly eighteen minutes after leaving Randolph Street.

Paul approached the man behind the desk hesitantly. "I came to inquire about the land for sale on County Road 97 near Redbud. Would you mind telling me how much it is selling for?"

John Logan shook his head and looked at Paul in disbelief. "Well, I'll be damned," he said, "are you psychic? The price for that property was reduced by fifty percent this very morning."

Apparently, John had been alone in the office for too many hours and was in need of someone to talk to. Gladly, he gave Paul and Senior the details concerning the sale of the land.

"On his death bed three weeks ago old man Graham put that property on the market for $30 dollars an acre. Two days ago, he died, making his son Alfred his executor. Just this morning Alfred called and said he was willing to sell the 200-hundred acre parcel of land for half the original price, provided the buyer agreed to pay the full amount in cash," John informed them. Then, he laughed heartily from the pit of his stomach and added, "I guess ole Alfie doesn't feel like screwing with his father's affairs; wants to get the ordeal over with. You could be one fortunate guy if you're interested."

Paul glanced at the clock on the wall telling him the time was 10:15. The Mercantile Bank & Trust closed at noon. If he hurried he could seal the deal that very day. "I'm going to tap my savings in Britt's Bay," he said tersely. "Dad and I will be back before you can prepare the paperwork."

Once the transaction was completed, Paul sighed deeply of satisfaction. It was turning out to be a good day after all; a very good day. He would share the news with Kathy on their date that same evening. He could hardly wait.

On the following Sunday, Paul, in blue jeans and a light tan pullover, left the apartment to go and pick up Kathy at her home in Redbud. On the drive there, flashes of lightening and loud claps of thunder followed in the wake of a light rain. At the Hollister House, he ran up on the front porch holding a large umbrella against the inclement weather. As he was about to use the knocker to announce his arrival the sound of Sarah's strident voice caused him to withdraw his hand and listen.

"Your Paul has a strong personality, Kathy. Don't let him lead you around like a puppy on a leash; assert yourself; be your own person," she advised her daughter.

"I agree that Paul is masterful and leads the way, but that's one of the things I admire about him. He doesn't dominate me, he takes care of me. Besides, it just so happens that I want the same things he wants; that's what makes our relationship so beautiful."

"Well, I certainly hope you are smart enough to make him wear a contraceptive when you have sex. I wouldn't want to see you saddled with a baby before you are even married."

"I'm sure Paul would love to hear that coming from you, mother," Kathy responded, particularly since we are saving our intimacy for marriage."

"Humph! I'll just bet you are!"

"Well, I've heard enough," Paul mumbled under his breath and used the knocker.

Exiting the house hurriedly, Kathy huddled against Paul under the umbrella and together they made a run for the car.

Once he was behind the steering wheel and she was seated beside him, he bent and planted a kiss on the puckered lips of her upturned face. "I couldn't help but overhear some of you and your mother's conversation. Eavesdropping is such a bad habit, I promise not to do it again; but thanks for defending me," he said with a wry smile, and then turned the key in the ignition and aimed the car for Britt's Bay.

"Mother can be a pain," she responded. "She must have been a real hell-cat before she married dad."

"Well, at least we know she wears a tarnished halo; it would be unbearable to live with a perfect angel."

Paul's remark caused Kathy to emit a spontaneous little laugh. "An angel mother is not," she declared, "believe me."

"By the way, you look stunning," he said. "The Briarwood clan is going to adore you."

When Paul ushered Kathy into his parent's home, background music from Scheherezade was playing softly. His father was stretched out in a recliner sound asleep, snoring quietly with his mouth open, his stocking feet propped up and his slippers askew on the floor. One hand was relaxed on the open page of a book on his lap. A pouch of tobacco, along with a clay pipe, sat in a bowl on an end table beside the chair. Someone had set up a card table next to the sofa and had started to work a jigsaw puzzle. A humming voice and the clatter of activity flowed from the kitchen area, along with the savory smells of fresh baked apple pie and mouth-watering pot roast.

Leaving his father undisturbed, Paul took Kathy's hand and led her into the kitchen where his mother was putting the finishing touches to the Sunday meal.

Clara's face lit up when she saw Kathy. Promptly, she stopped what she was doing, tilted her head to one side and proceeded to make a candid study of this slender young girl, standing familiarly next to her beloved son. She might have been a porcelain doll in a purple mid-calf skirt and a twin sweater set the color of lavender. The jewelry she wore was simple but tasteful. It consisted of gold button earrings and a fine gold chain from which dangled a gold shamrock the size of a quarter. In high heels, she reached to Paul's chin.

"Welcome to our home, Miss Kathy; Paul has been raving about you," she said and gave

Kathy a gentle hug and a motherly peck on the cheek. She then went on to explain that Paul's brother and two of his sisters would be coming to dinner with their families. "They're all anxious to meet you."

"It's a pleasure to meet you," Kathy said. "Is there anything I can do to help?"

"Not today, today you are the guest of honor," Clara told her. Then addressing Paul, she went on, "Why don't you show Kathy around the house before the others get here."

"It's only a house, Mom, what is there to see?" Paul retorted, as he silently compared the Hollister's posh interior with the more humble state of conditions in the Briarwood household. "However, there is something I want to show Kathy."

Steering Kathy across the living room, he took her to a portrait hanging above the mantel of the fireplace. "Meet my Grandfather Strong Bow Briarwood in his feathered headgear. He was a full-blooded Mowkatah Indian Chieftain. Do you know what that means?" he asked.

"It means that you are part Mowkatah Indian; you mentioned that in one of your letters. I didn't mind then, why should I mind now?"

"I think it may be the Indian blood in me that makes me think differently from many other men. I want you Kathy, but my principles deny me the pleasure of having you unless we marry. You are not a one-night stand. To take advantage of you would soil our relationship and rob it of its magic."

"Dear Paul, you wouldn't be the man you are without your grandfather's genes. I wouldn't change a thing about you if I could. Don't let mother's prattle upset you; you are all I want."

Putting his arms around her, he drew her to his chest and kissed her solidly. He might have proposed then, but the doorbell rang and the right moment vanished as his brother and his family made a noisy entrance.

Eventually, Paul learned to accept Sarah's brashness as a part of who she was. He found no fault with Joseph; their friendship solidified the day Joseph showed Paul his work shop in the carriage house.

"We continue to call it a carriage house, but I doubt that it has seen a carriage since the invention of the automobile," Joseph remarked. "Actually, it's a fancy three-car garage with a work area in the rear. Years ago the area was used to stable a horse and give a groom a spot to bunk down. My uncle converted the space into a work shop. I never saw a reason to change it."

A four-foot high wall partitioned off the work area from the three-car stalls to contain the wood shavings and sawdust created there. Two large peg boards displayed an assortment of tools of all sizes and shapes – hammers, saws, chisels, squares, levels, and so forth. A lathe, a table saw, a large work bench and a couple of smaller ones – one with a vise attached, and the other with a jig saw – were all there for Paul to drool over.

"I'm jealous!" he exclaimed, nodding at the framework of a four-drawer chest, standing on the work bench. The four drawers belonging to the piece had been set aside, ready for a final sanding. "I assume you are the craftsman?"

"I learned a bit about making furniture from my uncle. All of the joints are tongued and grooved. It'll be a fine piece when it's done, but it's taking me forever. I piddle away at it when I'm in the mood since it's such a nice relief after working with numbers all day long. When the weather is nice though, I'd just as soon be up on the mesa, making pictures in the clouds." He chuckled. "Guess I'm still a boy at heart. By the way Paul, if you need any of these tools for your job, you're welcome to borrow them. Many of the tools are primitive. You won't find any screwdrivers, sanders, or drills with electric cords in here. These take more muscle, but they still get the job done."

Although the Briarwoods and the Hollisters were not on a par in terms of wealth, the two families began to interact socially at events that usually involved food or celebration – dinners, holidays, barbecues, birthdays, and the like.

"Your parents are stimulating, Paul. Your mother Clara excels in the culinary arts and her pen and ink sketches are exquisite," Sarah raved between puffs on a cigarette. "I adore your father. The man is a marvel when it comes to nature. He can tell you at a glance if a weed is perennial, biennial, annual, noxious, medicinal or edible. And he has that resonant voice I could listen to all day."

After so many visits to the Hollister House, Paul was considered a part of the family. As a consequence, he became acquainted with the people who came and went frequently. Among them were the Hollister's next door neighbors, Edna and Sam Verducci and their daughter Peggy. Also, making the scene on occasion were farmer Jed and Nora Campbell and their son Jim. Soon, Paul felt at home with all of them.

A couple of weeks before Christmas, all ten of them shared an impromptu repast in the Hollister's kitchen; joking, exchanging light banter, and sipping red wine.

During the course of the evening, Jim and Peggy – who had been engaged to marry for some time – elaborated on the arrangements they were making for their wedding, which was to take place in January. The subject matter ignited a flame in Paul and made his passion for Kathy burn all the brighter.

When everyone else had departed, he lingered, determined to confront Joseph and Sarah about his feelings for Kathy. He was extremely conscious of the differences in their life styles and wouldn't blame them if they deemed him unworthy of her; and yet, what he had on his mind had to be aired.

Humbly, he took Kathy's hand in his and approached her parents. "Joseph, Sarah, I haven't the means to support Kathy in the fashion she enjoys here. All I can offer her is my undying love and a promise to make it up to her in the future. One thing is definite, I could never be happy without her. I've come to believe that she feels the same way about me. What I'm saying is, I'd like your permission to ask Kathy to marry me."

Reacting swiftly, Sarah left her seat, went to Paul, and surprised him with a big smack on the lips. "What took you so long handsome warrior? I've wanted you for my son-in-law from the first minute I saw you. If Kathy doesn't say 'Yes,' I'll divorce Joseph and marry you myself," she exclaimed. "In other words, you have my blessing. Oh, and Paul, as a reminder, my early tea roses will be blooming by April.

Joseph's blue, blue eyes – the same color as his daughter's – looked up from beneath bushy eyebrows and he raised himself up, assuming the courtly demeanor he displayed so well.

"You've said it all, my dear," he said to Sarah. "You're a fine man Paul; I've no doubt, you will do well by our daughter."

Overflowing with happiness, Paul turned to Kathy, his eyes brimming with emotion. He took her arm and said, "I think it's time for us to take a walk."

Under the satin darkness of a moonlit night, they strolled, arm in arm, on West River Road to the bridge that conjoined with North River Road. For a time they were engulfed in an easy silence, leaning on the railing and watching the waters of the river below rush past. Then....

"Paul, what are you thinking?" Kathy asked.

Taking her in his arms, he tucked a finger under her chin, tenderly raised her face, and looked into her eyes. "Only that I love you more than words can say; that I will always be faithful to you and hold you above all others; that I want to spend my life with you and have you bear my children. Other than my heart, I have nothing to offer you Kathy. I foresee lean days ahead, but I promise you, someday I will make you proud of me. With you by side, I will move mountains to reach my goal. Will you marry me, Kathy?"

"Yes, I will marry you Paul. You see, my love for you is a paradox. I feel that I could not love you more; and yet, each day I love you more than I did the day before. My love for you just grows and grows. I, too, will be faithful and hold you above all others. I will do all you ask of me and more. I will bear your children and dream your dreams."

"Then please accept this ring as a token of my love," he said and took a small black velvet box from a pocket and opened it to reveal a two-carat, square-cut emerald ring set in platinum. "On an impulse, I bought this in Nice, France with the winnings from a poker game. I had no idea then that your birthday is in June and that emeralds are the stone ancients chose for June births.

On Saturday morning, April 6, 1946, the clock tower in Redbud struck 10:00 as the bells in St. Bartholomew's Church steeple pealed loudly. Inside the church the altar was adorned with numerous candles and vases filled with dozens of yellow, pink, and white tea roses. Organ music played "True Love" softly in the background. Reverend P. Burkham stood poised on the altar, holding a book of prayer with his finger on the page containing the "Rites of Marriage."

Kathy, a paragon of loveliness in a white satin gown over-layered with Alencon lace and a fine-meshed finger-tip veil, stood sedately at the altar beside Paul, who was handsomely decked in a white tuxedo. The father of the bride, the best man, the ushers, the maid of honor, and the bridesmaids - made beautiful for the occasion - stood at their relative posts, waiting with the bride and groom-to-be, for the nuptials to begin.

The hush during the ceremony was broken only by Sarah's loud sniffles. Then when Reverend Burkham pronounced Paul and Kathy "Man and Wife," Sarah put her forefinger and middle finger to her teeth and blasted a shrill whistle, heard throughout the church. The gesture tickled Joseph. He rushed to give his wife an approving kiss and laughed gleefully.

Chapter V

THE HONEYMOON

Within minutes after the reception, Kathy and Paul were bumping north along a narrow, jagged route over high country. When they reached US-50, a modern four-lane highway, Paul put his foot to the pedal and headed west for their destination – a suite of rooms at the Blackthorn Lodge on the shores of Washtebah Lake in Tennessee.

Washtebah, a large, many-fingered lake just beyond the North Carolina border, spread out for miles along the highway. Midway, where the lake narrowed, engineers had built a bridge leading to the small town of Cutler's Corner. Blackthorn Lodge was situated in a wooded area nearby and overlooked the lake. Touted as a nature lover's paradise, the lodge promised access to a number of outdoor activities, fine dining and dancing as well as a lot of privacy.

When they arrived early in the afternoon a golden sun was shimmering on the riffling waters of the shallow lake. Deciduous trees in the surrounding wilderness etched the sky with leafy branches. The past autumn's leaves crunched underfoot as they made their way into the lobby of the lodge to claim their reservation. April was supposedly a slow period for the lodge-keeper; yet a handful of people were milling about, ogling them curiously.

Paul opened the door to the suite, picked up his bride and carried her over the threshold. "My Kathy, my wife, my beloved," he whispered hoarsely. With his heart pounding in his chest, he gathered her in his arms and kissed her again and again, tenderly and unhurriedly, unleashing sparks of passion that burst into flames and demanded fulfillment. He felt the heat in his wife's body; felt her respond in kind to his sensual starvation. Knowing that the first time would be painful for her, he wanted to bring her to the peak of arousal before penetrating her. However, he could not help his own surge of urgency. He undid the zipper on the back of her dress and let the dress fall to the floor then repeated the motion with his trousers. Now, his caresses probed more deeply, he explored more brazenly, and his kisses were more ardent. Finally, his appetite for her became unbearable. "Oh, my darling Kathy, I cannot wait. I must have you. Please, tell me you are ready."

Clinging to him, she molded her body to his. "Oh Paul, please, take me and make me yours; I love you, I love you so much!"

In frantic haste, they shed the rest of their clothing. Naked, he carried her to bed and made exquisite love to her. With bodies entwined and spirits meshed they built to an ecstatic climax so wonderful it shook the rafters of the gods. The gods were pleased and requested an encore. And then another.

It had been a long difficult wait, but now he was glad. They would always have this memory; this blissful time when they dwelt in heaven on earth and two souls fused to become one.

For the entire week, they belonged solely to each other; no one else shared their attention, time, or space. Whether in bed devouring each other, hiking the wooded trails, canoeing, horseback riding or dancing to a blue-grass band, they were enrapt only with each other. They held hands and watched sunsets; masterpieces painted with brush-strokes of gold, salmon, crimson and deep purple in a twilight sky; listened to the lulling sound of waves washing over the sandy shore. Any care they may have had was banished to some faraway place, and this tiny isolated Paradise was theirs to share.

All too soon, they were obliged to pack up and return to Britt's Bay to deal with the demands of life in the real world.

Still glowing from the magical moments they had shared while on their honeymoon, Paul and Kathy, arrived in Britt's Bay at dusk. The peak traffic hour had tapered off. Close to the vicinity of their apartment, in the downtown area, business places shone bright with lights and pedestrians milled about.

At the apartment building, Paul parked in his allotted space. Carrying their suitcases and newly acquired purchases, they went silently up to Apartment 23 and placed the articles in a corner of the living-room. After removing their outer garments, they automatically turned to each other. He took her in his arms, kissed her lightly on the lips, nuzzled his nose in her hair, and gazed lovingly into her eyes for a long moment before letting her go. Then, hand-in-hand, they stood quietly and surveyed their new home. The changes in their lives were drastic. For the sake of love they both had foregone the familiar to shape and share a life together in this small unfamiliar setting. They sat side by side on the sofa, kicked off their shoes, and again reached for each other. "I love you Mrs. Paul Briarwood, my darling wife; and I will love you until the end of time," he stated emphatically. "You are my all Kathy. You make me whole."

"What can I say, dear husband, when you've already said exactly how I feel about you."

"Are you hungry?"

"A little."

"Make do, or the deli around the corner?" he asked.

"A hot shower and make do," she replied.

"You know, Kathy, this place looks smaller than I remember. Even with that storage bin in the basement, we'll never fit the rest of our belongings in here. It is not as adequate as I thought. I'll have to leave my fishing and hunting gear with the folks for the time being. I suppose at the end of each work day I can lock my tools in the trailer Avery uses as his on-site office, which I really hate to do as they would cost a lot to replace if stolen."

Gradually, the newlyweds settled into a suitable routine, making sure there was time for socializing and for leisure on weekends.

In the heat of August Kathy felt the first impression of life in her womb. It was subtle, like an inch-worm wriggling in the lower left area of her abdomen.

One evening Paul came home from work to find her measuring the furniture in the bedroom.

"What are you doing?" The question was innocent enough; it was the answer that rocked him.

"Trying to see if we can fit a crib in here," she replied, and spinning around she threw her arms around him and put her head against his shoulder. "Paul, I felt it…., this morning…., a tiny little thing."

The Riddle of Kebor's Mesa

Taking her with him, Paul crashed on the sofa, held her tight against him and stroked her hair. For a long moment, he weighed their options, taking into consideration such things as their financial status, his job security, and their insurance coverage.

"Are you disappointed, Paul?" Kathy asked, breaking the silence.

"I'm elated."

"Then why are you so quiet?"

"I was just thinking. The first thing you are going to do is see an obstetrician Kathy; after that we're going house-hunting. We can't stay here; the place is too small and I won't have you running up and down three flights of stairs to do the laundry."

"Paul, we can't afford to buy a house."

"Dearest Kathy, we can't afford not to," he told her. "I'll talk to Avery; he'll know where we can get the most for our money."

On a Saturday morning in September, 1946, they moved into a modest cottage at 24361 Ingleside Avenue in a middle class neighborhood.

The Riddle of Kebor's Mesa

Chapter VI

DAVID AND MICHAEL

Kathy was in her second trimester of pregnancy when Senior retired and the elder Briarwoods moved to Redbud. For Kathy, the move was unsettling at first. She had become accustomed to her mother-in-law's comforting impromptu visits and relied heavily on her sage advice for expectant mothers.

However, since the cost of living was cheaper in Redbud, Senior's retirement annuity allowed him and Clara to have luxuries there that would have been unaffordable had they stayed in the city. Still, after residing in the same house in Britt's Bay for their entire marriage, they found the change of venue to the small valley town charged with apprehension. However, they soon learned that their fears had no basis, for life in the small town proved to be one of discovery and adventure.

"Outside my back door, about a half mile east of here there are woods loaded with game. And folks tell me the big lake south of the highway is full of bream and bass," Senior expounded to Paul and Kathy. "This was a good move."

He went on to show them where he planned to plant his garden, where he would build a shanty to house a couple of goats, and the space he would fence off for a chicken coop and a flock of Rhode Island Reds.

"This is what enriches me," he declared gravely with a wave of the hand that took in the acreage of which he spoke. "This is the life style I was born to live."

Clara was equally excited, but about different things. "Look, I have a dishwasher and modern cabinets and two bathrooms." She breathed a luxuriating sigh. "And, thank you God, no more stairs to climb to get to the bedroom."

The flowers in the fields took her breath away. The warmth of the people filled her heart. "When I shop, I am not just a stick figure with a purse hanging on my arm to the merchants, I am a real person."

At precisely 6:24 A.M., on Sunday, February 16, 1947, exactly ten months and ten days into the marriage, Paul witnessed the birth of his first son. While Kathy had endured agonizing labor throughout the night, he had alternated his time between pacing the corridors of St. John's Hospital and going to the birthing room repeatedly to check on her condition. The ordeal drained them both, but when it was over, they rebounded with surprising resiliency.

"And we shall call him 'Paul' for there is no denying that he is your son, dear husband, judging by his head of thick-black hair," Kathy observed.

"I prefer that he have a name all his own Kathy; Ralph or David or Robert...."

"David then; David Briarwood has a nice ring."

Gently, Paul took the tiny infant from Kathy and cradled it in his arms; his mind running rampant. My son, he thought, my precious son; will I be as good a father to you as mine is to me? Will I sense your needs and give you wise advice? Will I teach you to hunt and fish and swim?

At that instant he remembered that he had promised his father he would go "on-the-hunt" with him during open season. That's what men do, his father had said, they hunt and fish to put food on the table. Suddenly the old tradition of taking boys on the hunt at the age of fourteen seemed terribly important. His pulse quickened, recalling how thrilling the hunt had been – man against beast. Was there still time? Was the season still open? He didn't even know where his hunting gear was; or his fishing gear for that matter.

"Here's our little David, my love," he said and returned the bundle back to Kathy's arms. "It's time you got some rest. I'm going to Redbud to give our folks the good news, but I'll be back in a few hours."

In Redbud, he informed both sets of parents of the delivery of his newborn son and assured them that both mother and child were absolutely fine. At the Briarwood home, he had a second mission to fulfill. "Would you know offhand where my hunting gear is Dad?" he asked.

"Oh, are you telling me you are interested in going on the hunt this year?" Senior inquired with a tinge of sarcasm.

Paul countered the question with one of his own. "I feel good about the hunt again; the excitement and anticipation are back stronger than ever. I don't want to neglect Kathy, but do you see any harm in me getting up with the sun and squeezing in a few hours of hunting or fishing on a Saturday morning?"

"None that I know of," Senior replied. "You are my son Paul, of course you must hunt and fish. Your guns are on the shelf in the closet of the spare room along with your fishing gear. I was hoping you would find need for the rifle before the season came and went. We'll arrange to go on the hunt when it suits you and Kathy."

Kathy had no objections to Paul going hunting on a Saturday morning. It gave her an opportunity to spend time alone with their beloved infant; to coo to him, cuddle him, and talk baby talk.

Often, in the aftermath of Paul and Kathy's love making, relaxed and at peace with the world, they would cling to each other and express their innermost feelings. Together, they envisioned the building marvels Paul would create someday. Whether achievable goals, romantic whimsy, or merely chimera; the air-castle extravaganzas made their mediocre life style bearable and their outlook rosy. For Paul, the dream was like a beacon of light in a sea of uncertainty.

He realized that he had a long way to go to achieve the success he longed for. Looking to the future, he devoted long hours, five days a week honing his skills and gaining knowledge on the many facets involved with the construction of homes and buildings. On those idle days, when on-site construction shut down because of inclement weather or there happened to be a shortage of material, he experimented with the array of wood-working tools he had borrowed from the Hollister's carriage house, using his garage as a workshop. After he had gained enough confidence, and knowing he could call on Joseph if he needed help, he set out to make a chest of drawers for the nursery as a means of testing his developing skills.

As the scope of his capabilities increased, Avery compensated him accordingly. By March of 1948 Paul was recognized as a journeyman. The elevated status earned him a substantial wage increase and gave his ego a well-needed boost.

Meanwhile, David added a wonderful new dimension to their lives. Everything, it seemed, revolved around him. Pictures were taken of him at short intervals from the day he was born; one day old, three days, two weeks, a month, six months, his first-birthday. Every measure of progress was recorded with loving care; the day he first sat up, crawled, took a step, and said a word. They wouldn't part with him for all the gold in a king's counting room.

Even so, they freely confessed that parenting did not fit into any of their preconceived notions of all it entailed. Supposedly helpless, the infant had the maddening ability to create an amazing amount of work, redefining the meaning of colic and disrupting the routine and serenity of the household at any and all hours of the day and night. Fortunately, Kathy and Paul were generously endowed with a natural bent that

The Riddle of Kebor's Mesa

compelled them to love and nourish their offspring at all costs.

However, five days out of the week Paul put in an eight hour shift on the job and either studied late into the night or puttered with his woodworking tools in the garage, leaving the attendance to David's needs largely to Kathy. She found having to wash diapers on a daily basis especially troublesome.

Fortunately, Paul's pay increase permitted her to have diaper service for which she was especially thankful since she was due to deliver their second child. David, at nineteen months, was not yet potty trained.

At 7:06 AM, on September 22, 1948, a Wednesday, Michael Briarwood, another replica of Paul, made an appearance after nine hours of grueling labor.

By the time the delivery was over, Paul had sprouted the stubble of a black beard and looked as exhausted as his wife. Kneeling at her bedside, he brushed damp, limp hair from her face. "My dearest Kathy, I was hoping the second delivery would be easier than the first, but this little guy gave you a bad time, too."

She nodded, smiled feebly, and puckered up for his kiss. "I guess when you use the same formula, you get the same results," she said and smiled good-naturedly.

"Two sons…., they will hunt and fish with me, Kathy. Perhaps someday they will be my partners in business…." Then as quickly as he began to indulge in wishful thinking, he came back to the moment at hand. The dark shadows under Kathy's eyes made him wince, as did her pallor and weariness.

"I'm sorry you had such a bad time of it Kathy; God willing, this will be the end of it."

"Are you saying you don't want any more children, Paul? I know you hate the thought of using a condom, but I could have a tubal ligation through the vagina while I'm here. It would leave no scar."

"I want every child you give me, Kathy. You are the one who suffers, so how do you feel about it?"

"The pangs of childbirth are fleeting; the reward is great. It's the day to day care I'm concerned about. I don't want to become the wife who gets a headache every time her husband wants to make love to her. I want to be there for you."

"We don't have to make a decision right this minute. Let's give it some thought and maybe we can come up with a solution that pleases us both; and who knows, maybe God as well."

Paul awakened in the middle of the night with a foul taste in his mouth, coming out of a dream in which he had been sketching plans for a split-level house for his family. The plans called for a courtyard…. and a swimming pool…. and a…. Hastily, he got up and wrote down everything he could remember in a notebook. In the haze of his dream he seemed to be looking for a spot to put the crystal chandelier. Why would the crystal chandelier appear in his dream? Was there a hidden message in the context of it? Kathy had always been the one to make it sparkle merely because Sarah and the cleaning woman refused to touch it.

Of course, it dawned on him then that the solution to their problem had been in front of him all along; all he had to do was connect the dots.

He brought a bouquet of flowers up to the birthing room that morning and handed them to Kathy. "They remind me of you," he said, "a mixture of pretty colors and textures. David is doing fine with his Grandma Clara, but where is our youngest son? You haven't given him up for adoption, have you?"

"I nursed him, whispered sweet nothings in his ear, and handed him off to a pie-faced nurse for safe keeping."

"Good, because I have something to propose to you that he should not hear."

"Oh, and that is?"

"Suppose we carry on our love-life as we have since we married; I make mad love to you and you respond with reckless abandon with no worries about whether or not you are liable to get pregnant. If you should get pregnant with our third child, I promise you we will hire a nanny. Does that seem reasonable to you?"

Chapter VII

SARAH'S DEMISE

Time, that elusive element that waits for no man, flew by with unbelievable speed. Although he was now retired from the Army Corp of Engineers, Senior found pleasure in traipsing around the outskirts of Redbud with the critical eye of a surveyor. In the winter of 1951, he discovered where a rockslide from the face of the ridge east of the Limerick River had altered the course of the rainwater and snow-melt in that area. Instead of flowing into a gully on the far side of the ridge, most of the water now spilled over the scree toward the south. Several diverse trickles had converged to form a single rivulet that was gradually carving a path toward the river where the land formed a natural depression.

"Look at my hands Paul, all gnarled and calloused. I'm a humble man. I was born on a reservation and was lucky to get an eighth grade education in the public school system, but I know my job. I know the ways of gravity and the force of moving water. Spring rains will connect the narrow stream with the river and the river will top its banks; mark my words." Senior shook his head and went on to say, "I'd be remiss if I didn't alert the Army Corp of Engineers."

As Senior had predicted, in the spring of 1952 the Limerick River overflowed, flooding a section of the Campbell's farm. Having been forewarned, the Army Corp of Engineers had a flood control plan ready for execution. In August, heavy earth-moving machinery and cement-mixing trucks arrived on the scene to begin building a small dam.

Statistics showed that once the dam was completed, the waters diverted from the river would form a sizeable lake. This fact influenced the State of North Carolina's decision to build a State park that would encompass the lake and the acreage surrounding it. The plans included hiking trails, public facilities, camping grounds and more. In conjunction with the State's project, the roads in the area were scheduled to be upgraded to accommodate an anticipated increase in traffic.

The projected time frame was two years for the completion of the combined effort.

No one was more excited over the development than Paul; it meant that once the State Park was open to the public, the value of his property would appreciate dramatically. No one was more disenchanted than Sarah. She blamed the dust kicked up by the construction workers to be the cause for her watery eyes, scratchy throat, and difficulty in breathing.

Over-the-counter remedies gave her no relief. The symptoms continued to worsen. She began to complain of severe headaches, muscular pain, restlessness and lack of energy. Over and over again, Joseph urged her to seek professional help. She agreed that she should, but didn't. "It's probably an allergy, or a bug that's going around," she rationalized.

She rallied for the Christmas Holidays. Buoyed by the abundance of good cheer and excitement generated by family, friends and neighbors, she wrapped gifts, sent cards, sang carols, made dozens of cookies, and huge bowls of punch. She graciously greeted the visitors who came and went. On New Year's Eve, she and

Joseph played host and hostess to a boisterous crowd of revelers. Counting down the end of 1952, everyone ate, drank, and danced the night away.

Adrenalin kept Sarah afloat. She told bawdy jokes and flirted outrageously with every man there. At the stroke of twelve, she melted into Joseph's arms, kissed him soundly on the lips, and raised her glass of champagne with the rest of them to toast the New Year, singing "Auld Lang Syne."

Feeling the effects of champagne and eggnog, Paul slipped out the back door and went to sit at the base of an oak tree to clear his head and, hopefully, to settle his queasy stomach. In shadow and virtually invisible, he breathed deeply of clean fresh air.

A few minutes later, Senior exited the back door and began to walk toward the lane. Paul was about to ask him if he wanted company when Sarah dashed out of the house and ran to catch up with his father. "Senior, wait up, I want to talk to you", she called in a hoarse whisper and, reaching out, linked her arm through his.

"Sarah, is something wrong? What I can do?"

"Well, there is nothing wrong, but there is something you can do," she began, and then hesitated. "The trouble is, I don't know how to say what is on my mind," she told him conspiratorially and emitted a throaty chuckle. "Surely you know how much I admire you, Senior."

"And I admire you Sarah; you are a lovely lady and certainly a gracious hostess" Senior told her. "Just say what you have to say."

"It's difficult for me; I'm not in the habit of doing this…., but…., well, I want you to make love with me," she said and giggled. "There, I've said it. We can go to the carriage house. No one will know."

Paul watched his father stiffen and remove Sarah's arm from his. Facing her he said, "You and I would know; besides, what do you want with an old man like me?"

"You're still quite virile, I can tell. It would be our secret; just this one time," Sarah persisted and, placing her hands on his chest, looked up at him pleadingly.

"You've had too much to drink, Sarah," Senior rejoined and removed her hands. "I suggest you go back indoors and talk to Joseph about your needs. As for me, I am going to take a little stroll in the moonlight – alone. When I return, I'll dance with my wife and then we'll thank you for your hospitality and take our leave. This conversation will be forgotten."

Minutes after Sarah rejoined the party, Paul entered the house and, feeling betrayed by the woman he had come to regard with high esteem, glared at her accusingly.

Her eyebrows shot up and she stared back, fully aware that Paul had witnessed the dialogue she'd had with his father. Then, quickly she glanced away, unable to bear the hurt she saw in his eyes. She'd been foolish and regretted her actions, but that did not eradicate the damage she had done to her relationship with Paul. She doubted that he would ever look at her again with fond affection.

When the party was over and the last guest had departed leaving only the echoes and memories behind, she sat with Joseph on a sofa and assessed the mess; party favors and confetti strewn about, empty glasses, ice melting in buckets, and trays of food that had been picked over and left on the table. The scene depicted the remnants of a time that would never be repeated, that much she knew. The evening might have been perfect had she not tarnished it by submitting to a reckless desire to know Senior intimately. And she had no one to blame but herself.

The Christmas tree stood in a corner; still sparkling with tinsel, hundreds of glass ornaments, and multi-colored lights. It too, seemed redundant. Suddenly, she understood that the holidays had been a bright flicker from the candle of her life that had come and gone too swiftly.

Sarah considered the tree dolefully, reached for a cigarette from a pack on a nearby side table, lit it and inhaled deeply. The smoke made her cough violently. She took another quick puff, but rather than inhale, she exhaled the smoke instantly and snuffed the cigarette out.

"Why can't you quit, Sarah; those damn things are killing you," Joseph remarked harshly.

"I know, Joseph, I know, but you see, I do quit – every other day," she said, emitting a ragged little laugh at her own humor. "Everyone talks about the State Park incessantly. People seem to think it's going to put Redbud on the map. Humph!" she snorted, and then in an almost inaudible voice went on to say, "I wonder if I'll be here to see the day."

"Tomorrow, I'm taking you to see Doctor Leiberman. We'll get Minnie to come in and help clean up this mess," he said. "Later, if I have time I'll take the decorations down."

"Don't take the tree down, Joseph" she said on a whim, "leave it. Our holiday doesn't have to end here. The tree will make me feel good just to look at it."

As she spoke, Joseph went and scooped up a handful of pine needles from under the tree, threw them on the hearth and stoked the fire.

The Riddle of Kebor's Mesa

When he looked back, Sarah was gripping the arm of the sofa and gasping for breath.

"It's my back Joseph; an excruciating pain between my shoulders."

After being rushed to St. John's Hospital, she underwent a series of tests. The results of the tests came as a shock.

"Mr. Hollister, cancer is wide spread in both of Mrs. Hollister's lungs and elsewhere in her body as well," Dr. Leiberman told Joseph, "an operation would only hasten her death."

Often, during those final days, she considered telling Joseph about her lustful pursuit of Senior on the night of the party, but never quite got around to it. How could she tell Joseph of her wanton act and, in the same breath, convince him that he, and only he, was the love of her life? The other had been a stupid, irresistible wish for a last minute fling – nothing more.

Sarah Hollister died in her husband's arms on Friday, May 18, 1953. There were no death rattles, just a slight convulsion and a final audible emission of breath as her body collapsed and her spirit exited its earthbound housing.

Chapter VIII

KATHY AND PAUL MOVE TO REDBUD

Sarah's funeral was held in the afternoon the following Tuesday. The four-day time lapse was to allow relatives and friends living in Greensboro the opportunity to drive to Redbud for the services. Reverend Burkham of St. Bartholomew's presided, officiating with the same fervor he applied to all religious ceremonies. Roses from Sarah's garden decorated the altar of the church. Several eulogies extolled her many virtues. When it came Paul's turn to speak, he acknowledged her charm, her wit, her grace. She was a wonderful grandmother, he said, and a supportive mother-in-law. Unfortunately, as he spoke of her attributes, memory of her attempt to seduce his father overshadowed every good thing he had to say about her.

After the interment was over and a light meal had been served in the church's community hall, the mourners and condolers went their separate ways. To relieve David and Michael's impressionable young minds, Peggy and Jim Campbell took the boys to the farm where the topic of the day was more apt to be of the living rather than the tragedy of death. Kathy, Paul, and Joseph ambled slowly back to the old homestead, each contributing remembered tidbits about the woman who had been so much a part of their lives – Sarah Hollister.

Now Kathy and Paul sat in a glider and idly nudged it back and forth, heedless of its squeak. Drained emotionally and physically, Joseph sprawled in a lawn chair close to them. For the next half hour or so they continued to sing Sarah's praises; the same ones they had repeated over and over again since the seriousness of her illness had become known. Joseph smiled about her penchant for spending money on frivolous things.

Finally the subject of Sarah wound down. The three grievers grew silent for a spell. Sarah was dead and buried. The living had no choice but to go on living.

"Kathy and I would like you to come and live with us in Britt's Bay," Paul suggested to his father-in-law. "The boys can bunk together and you can have one of their rooms. You'd be near your work and you'd get to eat Kathy's good cooking,"

Joseph stared hard at Paul, and then at his daughter."You two are way ahead of me on this one. I had something similar in mind, but with another twist," he said. "It was your mother's wish that you live in this house with me. Frankly, there is nothing I'd like better. It would give you a chance to sell your house in Britt's Bay at a profit and get you out from under the steep interest rates you are paying on the mortgage. The only deficit I can see would be in the time you spend going to and from work, Paul; but then, that wouldn't amount to any more than a few minutes each way." Pausing to allow the wisdom of his logic to sink in, he eyed his son-in-law anxiously. Kathy would not need to be sold on the idea, that much he knew.

"Wait a second," Paul exclaimed loudly, putting his hands up in protest, "you're making a damn generous offer here, but I sure as hell am not looking for charity."

"Charity my foot, you'd be doing me a favor. This house needs people. It needs kids,"

Joseph persuaded. "You see, I've been thinking seriously that I might have to sell the house and, believe me, it's the last thing I want to do," Joseph explained.

Uncrossing her legs, Kathy got out of the glider and began to pace. "Exactly what do you have in mind for us, Daddy? Would we be renters, caretakers, or what?"

"Neither! You must understand that I can't let the house sit idle; it would fall apart in no time. I'd like you to move in, pay the taxes and utilities and treat the house and everything in it as your own. I intend to stay in a rented apartment in Britt's Bay during the week and come back here on weekends. All I'd ask is that one of the bedrooms be at my disposal. That's about it. Think it over and let me know."

Even as he spoke Joseph's eyes closed, his mouth popped open and he yawned widely. Fighting a strong urge not to wither in front of them, he stood up, arched his back and stretched this way and that; rolled his shoulders and flexed his muscles. "I'm sorry folks, I'm dog tired," he said, "I've got to get some rest. Perhaps we can discuss this further in the morning. And don't

The Riddle of Kebor's Mesa

forget, I'll want to see my grandsons before you go back to Britt's Bay."

He started for the back door, then turned and offered Paul his hand. "It would be a gentleman's agreement."

Accepting the handshake, Paul rose to his feet and nodded. "I'll let you know."

After Joseph had gone to bed, Kathy and Paul took a leisurely stroll along West River Road in the dim light of a fading sun. Shoulders brushing, engaged in separate thoughts, all was quiet except for the dissonant din of tree frogs and crickets serenading the onset of night. Then,

"My dear Kathy, wouldn't it be foolish of me to ask if you want to move back into the old homestead?" Paul asked at length.

"It would," Kathy admitted, and laughed lightly. "Is it that obvious?"

"The house has been neglected for a few years, Kathy, and there is nothing wrong with the house we have in Britt's Bay."

"We have a lovely house in Britt's Bay, but Britt's Bay is not the valley," Kathy countered. I love the history of the old homestead; and the nooks and crannies and the rich wood moldings you don't find in modern houses."

"Hmm, well, come to think of it, I first saw you in front of the old relic, so maybe I am indebted to it, after all."

"Are you saying what I think you're saying?"

"I am not exactly thrilled with the prospect of living in the Hollister House, but I can see how it would benefit us financially; so yes, we'll take your father's offer. To compensate him, I'll do what I can do to restore the place to its original condition. Of course, some things will need a woman's touch; that's where you will come in Kathy."

"Perhaps the move is meant to be Paul; the timing is perfect. We can start getting ready, and then when the school year ends for David, we'll be set to go. Thank God, our boys are old enough to fend for themselves; I can foresee a few years of work ahead of us if we are to resurrect the old place."

"You know I loved your mother Kathy, but her sense of décor was not mine." Yes, he had loved Sarah, but he had seen a side of her that disgusted him. He wished it were not so, but now when he thought of her all he saw was the blot on her character.

"Nor mine."

Their walk had taken them to their usual stopping point – the bridge that spanned the Limerick River and connected West and North River Roads. They turned around there and traced their steps back to their starting point. Quietly, they let themselves in the back entrance and tiptoed up the rear stairs. Once they had gained the privacy of their bedroom Kathy began to sob uncontrollably.

Haltingly, she tried to explain the reason for her tears. "Mother is dead, I'll never see her again; and yet, because of her all of this is ours. I've no right to be so happy."

Paul reached out and put his arms around her. With her head on his shoulder, she wallowed in the intimacy they shared. The climate of the sad event discouraged even the thought of intercourse; it simply was not the time or place for a sexual encounter. However, of its own volition, arousal occurred and they ended up in bed making love; poignant and deeply satisfying love.

Long after Paul had fallen asleep, Kathy lie thinking about the monumental task they were undertaking. The move itself would only be the beginning. Bringing the house back to prime condition probably meant rewiring the place, insulating the outside walls, and updating the plumbing. The white paint on the house had weathered and was now the shade of pewter. It was beginning to flake in spots. A shutter was missing; another hung askew. Most of the windows needed to be re-puttied. Jimsonweed crowded the daisies and daylilies. Canada thistle encroached on the roses and azaleas. The front and back lawns were rife with dandelions. Remedy those problems and there was still the interior to consider.

Sarah had been a spendthrift, obsessed with collecting every trinket and gaudy gewgaw that grabbed her fancy. Without rhyme or reason she had interspersed the cheap and ugly with articles of real value throughout the house. As a result, her penchant for flamboyance often exceeded good taste and did not necessarily perpetuate the theme for elegance that had been established in the Hollister House decades earlier.

Without quite realizing it, she had created a museum of sorts; a crazy quilt of motifs and ideas that were uniquely hers. In effect, the woman who had been Kathy's mother lived on in the visual images she left behind from the cellar to the attic.

Kathy vowed to cherish her mother's memory forever; however, Sarah's presence must be eradicated from the house. If she and Paul were to live happily in the Hollister House then their personalities, not Sarah's, had to be reflected in it.

With that thought in mind Kathy finally drifted off to sleep, unaware that she carried a fertilized ovum in her womb, the cells of which were dividing with unbelievable rapidity; one becoming two; two becoming four, and so forth. Still, the developing mass at that stage was so microscopically small; it could be accommodated on a pinpoint.

The newly engendered bit of life was, of course, oblivious to the idea that it contained the blueprint for complex intelligence and human form, that its destiny was already in the making, and in nine months it would be properly named William Briarwood.

He would be called Billy.

Chapter IX

THE RESTORATION OF THE HOLLISTER HOUSE

The following morning, still wearing his pajamas, Joseph went into the kitchen to make coffee with Sarah's last wish foremost on his mind. It was the first thing he mentioned when Kathy and Paul came sauntering in, fully clothed, a short time later. Without so much as a "Good morning," he backed away from the refrigerator, where he had been poking around to see what was on hand to eat, and began to talk. He talked fast and non-stop until he had said everything he wanted to say.

"Did I tell you everything in the house would be yours to do with as you wish, Kathy? And the work shop would be yours to use exclusively Paul; I don't intend to spend any more time making furniture. I'll have someone re-putty the windows, repair the shutters and paint the house – any color you choose. The orchard needs to be cleaned up as well; I'll see to that. You see, it was your mother's dying wish that you live in this house. As a parting gesture to her, I'll do anything to get you to agree to move in."

"Are you through ranting, Daddy?" Kathy asked kindly as she placed a carton of orange juice on the table.

"We've already decided to move in Joseph, you don't have to sweeten the pot. I'll take care of the repair work; it's the only way I can repay you for your generosity," Paul told Joseph and tendered his hand to seal the deal.

"Whew! Believe me, that's a big load off my mind. I hope the move will be soon," Joseph said, reaching into the cupboard for coffee cups. "There's bread for toast, and eggs if either of you are interested."

"Kathy, if you'll set the table, I'll make breakfast this morning," Paul volunteered.

Moving with unconscious effort, Kathy set about to do Paul's bidding before answering her father. "We won't move until the end of the school year, Daddy, but in the meantime we'll probably be here on weekends. And I'll try to come in one or two days a week to do some work around here. There's a lot to be done; which reminds me....." she began, and then leaving a handful of utensils in a pile on the table, she went to Paul, turned him toward her, placed her hands on his upper arms, and gave him a 'me wife, me-want-something-from-husband' look.

"Do you remember telling me you would hire a nanny to help me with the housework if we had a third child?" she asked, looking cross-eyed at his open collar and the wild black hair standing out from the thin mass on his chest. Should I pluck that rogue? She pondered the idea briefly, and then sighed; no, better leave it for later.

"Yes, I do remember making that promise, but we don't have a third child. Michael will be celebrating his fifth birthday in a few months so it doesn't seem likely that we were meant to have another youngster, Kathy. What's the catch?"

"Well, you've got to admit, this is a big house to take care of and I was wondering if, instead of a nanny, you would let me keep Minnie to help out?"

"Who is Minnie?" Paul asked.

"The cleaning lady, she's very dependable. Mother had her for years."

"Funny, I never heard her called by name before."

"Minnie Gibson is her name. She is a widow who lives in the little yellow house on the other side of the highway."

"If I say 'Yes,' will you let me get on with our breakfast? I need to call Dad and let him know I won't be going fishing with him and Mark this weekend."

"Paul, you should go, there's plenty to keep me busy until you get back."

"No, I want to help, but if I know David and Michael they will want to go fishing with their Grandpa Senior and Uncle Mark; if that's okay with you."

"Yes indeed! Gosh, I don't know what I'd do with a baby in diapers right now."

Without a twinge of guilt, Kathy retained Minnie's services on Thursdays and hired a local handyman to lend a hand when needed. The first order of business was to remove the ashtrays from every room in the house and trash them. The mattress Sarah had slept on was also earmarked for disposal. The master bedroom furniture, of antique stock and irreplaceable, was taken up to the attic to be stored for posterity.

And so it went, bit by bit inferior articles of furniture were weeded out from among fine quality antiques and pieces that had been handcrafted by Joseph and his uncle. The furniture of lesser quality would find its way to a charity or be discarded. The showcase pieces of furniture would be incorporated with the quality articles she and Paul intended to bring from Britt's Bay.

Throughout the house, heavy velvet and brocade draperies, aged and laden with dust, were taken down and discarded. Later, when time allowed, using her own sense of creativity and sewing expertise, Kathy planned to replace them with sheer chiffon window treatments the color of ivory.

The walls were stripped of flowery wallpaper and painted with satin-finish earth tones. Lighting fixtures were replaced. Some of the overstuffed furniture was earmarked to be re-upholstered.

Many of the ornamental eyesores and gimcracks were included in a load of extraneous household goods destined to be sold to a used furniture dealer; a few of undecided worth were hauled up to the attic. The crystal chandelier kept its place over the dining room table.

On most weekends Paul and Kathy were both on the premises. Frequently, Paul worked outdoors or in the carriage house; tweaking the workshop layout in an attempt to make it more efficient for his particular purposes.

And because his "someday" dream for success was never far back in his mind, he often set aside a half hour or so to bicycle to the site of his 200 acre parcel of land just so he could breath in the essence of it and keep the dream alive. When allowed more time, he would bring a pad and pencil with him and roughly sketch the home he intended to build on a specific plot of ground.

Mainly, innovative designs for homes came to him from two separate sources; his own imaginings and the many forms of architecture used for dwellings around the world throughout the years. Visibility was important to him. He incorporated spacious rooms, half walls, and glass enclosures into his designs. He had a yen for classical fireplaces and fireplace chimneys. Also, his version of asymmetrical as well as symmetrical roofs almost always featured dormer windows and generous overhanging eaves. The homes he had in mind would not only have eye appeal; but would be creature comfortable, functional, and pleasant to live in.

With every day that went by, he saw his someday dream draw closer to reality. Someday his dream would be today.

Chapter X

KATHY AND PEGGY COMMISERATE

In five short weeks most of the cosmetics in the Hollister House were completed, school was out for the summer, and the Briarwood house on Ingleside had been put on the market. On Saturday, June 19, 1953, the young Briarwoods packed the last of their belongings and changed their venue from Britt's Bay to Redbud to set up housekeeping and rekindle old friendships.

Born months apart, Margaret (Peggy) Verducci and Kathleen (Kathy) Hollister had been close friends all their lives. When Peggy married Jim Campbell and Kathy married Paul Briarwood, they became a tight-knit foursome. Peggy and Jim lived on the Campbell farm with his parents, Jed and Nora.

The Riddle of Kebor's Mesa

Because thus far the young couple had been unable to produce offspring of their own, Peggy and Jim delighted in having David and Michael spend the day with them and sometimes the night, as had been in the case on the day of Sarah's funeral.

Needless to say, Peggy was ecstatic about Kathy's return to the valley. She began to pop in routinely on weekday mornings. "Just for a minute," she'd say, and then stay for tea or coffee and chat up a storm with Kathy while they nibbled on scones or sugar-coated doughnuts.

One morning Peggy showed up all atwitter and starry-eyed. She let herself in, a habit she had acquired a long time ago, and sat at the table, fingering the collar of her sleeveless cotton print sheath, obviously bursting with excitement.

"Let me guess, you've got a new foal," Kathy said.

"Better!" Peggy exclaimed.

"Ah, I know, Jim hit the lottery!"

"Better, Kathy, better!"

"Oh, just spit it out, before you choke on it."

The Riddle of Kebor's Mesa

"I'm two weeks late, Kathy," she said emphatically. "I'm two weeks late and you know what that means; I might be pregnant. Oh, God I hope I am. I had to tell you. I don't dare tell Jim, not until I've seen the doctor and I'm sure."

"Your body gives you signs, Peggy. Are your breasts beginning to swell....?" Kathy began to explain the early signs of pregnancy; then, her eyes opened wide. She stopped talking and placed her hands on her own breasts. "Oh, my God!" she exclaimed, "I've got to check the calendar." Dropping a half-eaten piece of pastry on a plate, she bounded for a wall calendar tacked inside a cupboard door. After tracking the dates back to her last menstrual period she spun around and regarded her friend with astonished eyes; her complexion a sickly shade of green.

"Is something wrong, Kathy?"

"I'm going to throw up," she replied and ran for the nearest bathroom. Minutes of retching went by before she returned to the kitchen, wearing a silly grin. "I'm nine weeks overdue. How did I ever miss two periods without knowing, Peg? Where on earth does time go?"

The Riddle of Kebor's Mesa

"Are you saying you're pregnant?" Peggy asked, wanting confirmation.

"I am definitely pregnant," she answered, her hands again going to her breasts. "I was ready for David and Michael, Peg. I'm not sure I'm ready for this one." She tucked a strand of hair behind an ear and blinked pensively into the distance. Then, "Thanks for sharing with me, Peg, I didn't mean to rain on your parade. It's just that I'm in a bit of a shock. I hope you are pregnant, too, so our kids can grow up together just like you and I did."

Paul, too, felt the shock waves. He'd resigned himself to having two sons that he absolutely adored. So, it took a few minutes for him to absorb the reality of Kathy's unexpected news; news she delivered in a roundabout way.

"I need a vacation," she told him matter-of-factly as she struggled to get out of her undergarments in the privacy of their bedroom that night.

"I thought we had agreed to take the boys to Epcot in August," he reminded her as he, too, undressed down to his skivvies.

The Riddle of Kebor's Mesa

"Why can't we go to the mountains next week, just for a few days. I need to be where all I have to do is look at the scenery and bird watch," she suggested, slipping a nightgown over her head.

"I'm lucky to be getting two weeks off to go to Florida, but we've gone over this before Kathy; you know summer is our busiest time of year. Why not ask Minnie to see to David and Michael instead; go shopping, have lunch out, buy some new clothes."

"That won't cure what ails me, Paul." she said, "Look at me, look at my boobs."

"Yeah, they're nice, I like them very much. What has that got to do with anything?" he asked, looking baffled.

Going to him, she positioned her still slim young body within an inch of his tanned muscular torso and, hands on hips, face in a queen-size pout, she tilted her head back and looked him in the eye. "We're going to have a baby."

Paul's reaction was not the least genteel. "No shit!" he said.

The Riddle of Kebor's Mesa

When the news finally sunk in he laughed, much to Kathy's chagrin. "It isn't funny," she told him.

"It's hilarious. It's poetry on a grand scale. Now you have a legitimate excuse for hiring a nanny."

As much as Kathy missed her mother, she was glad that Sarah was not there to needle her about having another "little Indian" as she was apt to say if Paul were out of earshot. Fortunately, for the developing fetus, her motherly instincts were sound. Like snow crystals falling on a hot rock, the resentment she felt initially evaporated with the first flutter of life.

Chapter XI

BILLY IS BORN

At seven o'clock in the morning on Wednesday, February 10, 1954, a widespread rainstorm drenched the valley. Lightning flashed, thunder sounded, and the wind blew strong. The electricity blinked off and on in the Hollister homestead.

Since Kathy was due to deliver, Paul decided to stay home from work. He made breakfast. Afterward, he drove David and Michael to school. When he returned home, Kathy had gone into labor. Her pains were less than ten minutes apart, so there was no time for a trip to the hospital in Britt's Bay. Frustrated and scared, he used profanity unlike any he had ever used before, even when in the Army.

Contained chaos followed. Desperate, Paul phoned his mother and Minnie Gibson and asked them to come and help with the delivery. Coming from opposite ends of town, the women came in separate cars at once; all aflutter, dressed in rain gear and carrying big umbrellas.

While Minnie manned the telephone to obtain minute by minute instructions from Doctor Davenport in Britt's Bay, Paul and Clara worked with Kathy. After forty-five minutes of intense drama the baby was born; healthy and sound, red and wrinkled, squinty-eyed and kicking as the grandfather clock under the staircase chimed the quarter hour –10:15 AM.

By the time everything had been cleaned up and put in order the storm had subsided. Clara and Minnie departed, leaving Paul alone with his wife and newborn.

"He may not be another image of you, but he is beautiful just the same. With that shock of red hair and baby blue eyes - that I am certain will be green within months - he reminds me of mother." She put her lips to the baby's tiny forehead. "Why do you show up now, precious one, when I have so little time to give you?" she asked of the swaddled bundle in her arms. Then, glancing up at Paul, she mistook the dumbstruck look on his face to be the result of the ordeal he had just been through. She gave him a dimpled smile. "I know this has been difficult for you husband, and I'm sorry you didn't get your girl, but would you happen to have a name for another boy?" she asked in dulcet tones.

On two previous occasions, the sight of God's miracles, the products of his seeds, had given him the highest high he ever hoped to achieve. This third child evoked no such sense of elation. By rapid calculations, the child had been conceived about the time of Sarah's death. Could it be she? come back to haunt him?

Feeling a detached kind of warmth for the child, he picked it up in his arms and began to pace the floor; mostly because it was expected of him. He studied the tiny face - so sweet and innocent - and filled his lungs, wishing fervently that he felt the same depth of love for this red-haired infant that he did for David and Michael. For some ungodly reason the tainted essence of Sarah blocked the way. Even as he vowed to make every effort to treat him fairly, he knew in his heart that the fathering of his third son would be reserved; stilted. Of course, he might feign a love he didn't feel, but that would be pointless;

kids from the earliest stage had a way of seeing right through deception.

"I had been thinking in terms of 'Wilma' had it been a girl, so why not name him 'William?'"

"Fine, we'll name him 'William,' but we will call him Billy."

Chapter XII

BILLY IN THE FIRST PERSON

Imagine if you will an infinitesimal embryo, enveloped in the dark folds of its mother's womb, warm and secure, soothed by the rhythmic sounds of her bodily functions, developing over a nine-month period, phase by phase, into a four-limbed creature. At the critical moment of emergence, it is without power or reason; without references or emotions. The only impression on its brain is one of awakening; a growing awareness of being. Then, suddenly it is thrust into a cold hostile atmosphere, stripped of familiar sounds and the protection of its mother's moist chamber. It is held by the ankles, made to unfold its tiny arms and legs, slapped and made to cry, to fill its lungs with a foreign substance, then doused with oil and water. It is probed. Then, at last the birth pangs are over for the infant as well as for the mother. Cleansed of foreign matter, it is wrapped in swaddling clothes and handed to its mother to be nourished and comforted.

The above describes the course I might have taken on my journey from conception to delivery. I would remember none of it except the utopian blackness of mother's womb and of becoming aware; surprised by the gift of life and the sensation of effortless movement at the instant of emergence. Not that I could verbalize any of it for I had no vocabulary; it just WAS. That very first experience of life left an indelible imprint on my brain. As my thought processes developed the event became increasing clear. Often in the years ahead I would puzzle over my birth and try to remember who I was and where I was before I became William Briarwood.

At birth, Dad had seen the image of Grandma Sarah in my coloring and it disappointed him. I became his special child; an unwanted treasure he had received with no return label; one he must treat with extra care lest he appear ungrateful.

Mother, too, beheld me as a symbolic re-entrance of Sarah into her life, but accepted me as a pleasant reminder of the woman who had given birth to her; not as someone who would be a constant reminder of a moment in time that had gone sour.

For Mother, being homemaker at 117 Nutmeg Lane was an affair of the heart; a romantic attendance to domesticity. Uppermost in mind was the need to make and keep a snug haven for the family unit; a harmonious nucleus that would draw her loved ones back to the hearth from wherever they might roam. She had known, even before I was born, that time spent to properly mother me would prevent the fulfillment of those wifely pursuits. If left unresolved, eventually my interference would shorten her temper and sharpen her tongue; thus creating discord she'd find hard to tolerate. For that reason, she acted on Paul's promise of a nanny. With great reluctance, she surrendered my care to Minnie for a portion of each day during the week.

"Aunt" Minnie, as I came to know and love her, had a ready smile punctuated with a gap left by a missing front tooth. She wore tennis shoes and ankle socks with ill-fitting dresses; too tight across her ample bosom and too loose around her hips. I saw her as an angelic figure in comic relief.

The childless widow's maternal instincts were raised to a conscious level the moment she witnessed my arrival; a feeling reinforced by her involvement. Enriching her existence tenfold, I became the son she never had.

It was Aunt Minnie who recorded my milestones; my first tooth, first step, first word. As though I were an exotic orchid, she watched over me as I learned to walk and talk, to eat and dress, and to run and play. Her care-giving often included Stephen and Susan, the twins Peggy Campbell gave birth to approximately two months after I was born.

The twins and I became as close as siblings. I began to spend an increasing amount of time on the farm with them under the care of Cora, their grandmother. Gradually, I was eased out of Minnie's keeping. When I reached the age of four, her services as my nanny ended; however, the bond between us remained strong and she continued to be my surrogate aunt.

Minnie Gibson was only one of many who influenced my formative years. I looked forward to Grandpa Hollister's weekly visits. With each one, my fondness for him grew. Even as a toddler,

I sensed the sadness behind the twinkle in his eyes and puzzled over the meaning in the message he sometimes telegraphed to Mom and Dad while mussing my red hair. However, no one affected my thinking and behavior more than my parents. I would never intentionally do anything to hurt or dishonor them.

A year or so after I was born, the State Park opened officially to the public and people from Redbud and the surrounding towns as well were enjoying the amenities it had to offer. As a result of the park's popularity, the scenic beauty in the area began to generate interest where little had existed before.

Early in 1958, a MacDonald's fast-food restaurant sprouted at the intersection of County Roads 97 and 86. Shortly thereafter, Shell Oil constructed a full-service gas station across from the water tower. At the same time, plans to widen the highway to four lanes moved from under the microscope of public officials to become an actuality, causing property value in the area to spiral upward.

With renewed enthusiasm, Dad decided to develop a ten-home subdivision close to the highway on his 200 acre parcel of land. Each house would feature a one-of-a-kind elevation based on his creativity. Cookie-cutting, he said, was best left to homemakers in the kitchen. However, he needed help; a lot of help from the right sources. He turned to his father-in-law Grandpa Hollister, and to Avery Pomeroy.

Through Joseph, Dad procured a loan from the Mercantile Bank & Trust Company to finance the project; and then teamed up with Avery.

Avery was the perfect man with whom to form a partnership. He had legal knowledge concerning mortgages, contracts, employee's entitlements, building permits and so forth. He had inside ties to suppliers, crews of able men, a fleet of trucks and other heavy equipment. And, he was completely receptive to the idea.

Although Paul's original plans had been to form a partnership with his two sons *someday* - not with Avery or anyone else - he found that dreams change shape with the passage of time. Under the circumstances, he fully appreciated Avery's involvement for he could not have undertaken the project alone, and it was the project that brought him closer to his life's goal.

Chapter XIII

BILLY, A SEEKER OF TRUTH

Despite our age differences – David being eight years older and Michael six years older than I – Mother and Dad were instrumental in developing strength of character in me every bit as much as in my brothers. As parents, they strived to set good examples for all three of us. They gave us solid moral standards to live by and were strict when necessary. In addition, on and off through my formative years, Dad taught me everything he understood about the mysteries of the universe, about meditation, and the importance of keeping an open mind.

"Meditation is a form of prayer in which you consciously will your mind to go blank, allowing your personal God to communicate with you. It's as simple as that," he explained in one instance.

The fact that I was destined to be a seeker of truth didn't manifest itself all at once, but stole upon me as gently as thistledown, nudging my thoughts by degrees over a period of time. Dad's proclivity to meditate was reason enough for me to emulate him. His profound thinking about the unknown became the basis for the questions I would ask later in life; questions to which there were no apparent answers. Only in looking back did I realize that even as a child I had a pensive side that responded to an undeniable urge to slake an insatiable curiosity; to know more profoundly the Divine Power that controlled all things visible and invisible.

I began to absorb notions pertaining to the God-force early on. From wispy impressions, God emerged as a concrete being when I was four. I saw Him as the proverbial Great-Grandfather figure with long white hair and a beard that flowed whichever way the wind blew. Robed in loose folds of white diaphanous fabric, He sat on a pearl-studded throne in heaven. Obscured by billowy white clouds, He gazed upon the whole of creation with fierce all-knowing eyes. Simultaneously, in some mystical way, He was eternally present; a heavenly guardian and protector, understanding my every thought, motive and desire; a God-father who loved me unconditionally and would not steer me wrong.

Although the concept was tragically naïve, it was blissfully comforting. But then, in those grand and golden days of childhood my comprehension did not demand that black be proven black, nor white be proven white. Without prejudice or guile, I luxuriated in the diversities that life had to offer, accepting whatever happiness came my way in however small packages.

Now, without Minnie to trace my footsteps I began snooping in the cubbyholes and storage closets around the house on a quest for hidden treasure. Months of searching through the things that people can't bear to part with but never use, I came up with a white oilcloth cat with leather whiskers, a toy garden rake, a book of cutouts and a pair of toy scissors; items that would gladden any child's heart.

After I had rearranged just about everything in the cubbyholes and storage closets in the house that I could find, I turned to the attic. I'd seen people carrying articles up into the attic and come away empty handed, so it made sense that mini worlds existed beyond the attic door. Eager to see what kind of "stuff" was there, I clambered up the stairs clutching the neck of Garibaldi, my stuffed giraffe.

Effectively, the attic was an enormous storage room with dormer windows on all four sides of the house. The walls exposed plastered laths. A network of rafters crisscrossed overhead. Planking covered the entire floor, giving you the notion that the area had been intended for living quarters at one time.

Articles used periodically were stashed near the head of the rear staircase – Christmas decorations, folding chairs, and luggage; trunks containing extra blankets and linens, and the like. Items kept for possible future needs, were stored near the front of the house. The heirloom furniture was protected with dust covers and stored in a separate corner.

Yet another heap of articles, stored under the eaves in the farthest reaches of the attic, appeared to be an accumulation of several generations of Hollister's old, so-called treasures; everything from a rusting birdcage and a dressmaker's form, to wicker baskets, dated magazines, and stacks of boxes filled with old clothing, lace-up shoes and feathered hats.

I was drawn to a carton of buttons and beads partially concealed by a crumpled tarpaulin that lie in the foreground. In an attempt to dislodge the carton I began to tug at it with all my might. To my surprise, it popped loose suddenly, and the contents went flying. Enchanted, I watched, one, two, three crystal beads the size of marbles, slowly make zigzag lines across the attic floor. They came to a halt in a shaft of sunlight.

I thought that I had unearthed three terrific glass marbles; more beautiful than any I kept in a bag in my room; too beautiful to be played in a game where they might get chipped or lost to a player. I had to have them; they were items to be held, admired and, like a pirate's cache of gold, concealed from prying eyes. Greedily, I put them in my pants pocket along with a skeleton key and an Indian-head penny I had also chanced upon.

Unfortunately, I forgot to take them out of my pocket when I changed my clothes, leaving them to be found by Mother. Of course, she questioned me.

"Where did you get these, Billy?" she asked.

"In the attic, mom; they were mixed in with some buttons and beads," I answered.

"Hmm, that's strange; they should be in a lidded tin can with the rest of them," she commented. "Oh, well...."

"Mom, can I keep them, please?"

"These are replacement beads for the crystal chandelier in the dining room. They are made of Austrian crystal and are very old and precious. They are not toys."

"I'll take good care of them; honest."

She looked at me with uncertainty, glanced at the beads, rolled them around between the palms of her hands, then said, "Oh, here, put them in your pocket and don't lose them. If you find any more bring them to me." Then, in a spontaneous gesture, she picked me up and swung me around, hugged me and kissed the top of my head. "I love you, my little green-eyed monster. Now go and play and stay out of that attic."

I heard her say as plain as day to "go and play," but the tail end of the sentence went unheard; the attic lured me back again and again. It became a place to while away the time on a rainy day; a calming room where childish peeves might vanish in picture albums.

When I tired of poking through things, I sometimes sat and gazed out of a dormer window, selecting it according to my mood. One afternoon I chanced to look out of the dormer window facing north and saw multiple mountain peaks not visible from the valley floor. From my lofty perch, the mountains appeared to roll on and on toward the horizon until they disappeared into a misty void. Somehow the scene reminded me of the velvety void from which I emerged at birth.

Several times I tried to share the knowledge of my birth with my family; tried to explain what I knew to be true; but no one would believe me - not Mother, Father; David or Michael. When Michael made a joke of it and laughingly remarked, "Billy, you're still in the dark," and everyone laughed with him, I knew then that some things are meant to be shared with God alone.

Within my limited capacity to reason, I felt certain that there were people somewhere in the world with similar perceptions of their births; perhaps in the far reaches of the mountain mist. Was it possible that the mountain mist held the secret to where I had been before awakening? These were some of the thoughts I had as a naïve little boy seeking answers to a hazy, but seemingly real recollection. However, I did not have the staying power to dwell overly long on such grim matters. When a flock of birds began to soar above Kebor's Mesa, my thoughts turned to them. Relegating everything else to the back of my mind, I focused on the circling, diving, sweeping motions of the birds until, as if on cue, they all took flight and disappeared from sight.

My fascination with the mountains had only begun. In the quiet of a lazy summer Sunday afternoon Grandpa Hollister sat in the glider in the yard and casually applied sandpaper to a cricket box he was fashioning for me while he reminisced about the days of his youth. Enrapt, I sat cross-legged on the ground and listened. It wasn't long before the subject of the mountains came up.

"Why, I used to come to the valley when it was no more than a burg. George Clawson ran a Post Office from the back of a grocery store. Sam and Edna Verducci were here, and so was the Campbell Farm. Sam, Jed and I used to spend our summers horseback riding and climbing mountains. Kebor's Mesa was our second home. We camped out on it whenever Jed's daddy would give him a couple days off from farm work."

"I can see some of the mountain peaks from the attic window, grandpa."

Joseph put the block of wood and sandpaper aside to study my upturned face. I was wearing tennis shoes with no socks, a pair of blue shorts and a plaid shirt, buttoned out of kilter. "Are the mountains calling to you, Billy?"

I shrugged. If they were, I didn't hear them. "Which mountains did you climb grandpa? Can you see them from here?"

"You can see mountains everywhere you look when you are driving through North Carolina, but for a really good look at the mountains in this area, the best place to go is to the summit of the mesa. I guess I climbed all of the closest ones, one time or another."

"Grandpa, take me with you the next time you climb the mesa. I want to see the mountains from up there."

"You're a bit young yet, Billy. Your mother was nine years old before I took her up with me."

"You mean Mom climbed to the top of the mesa? Wow!"

"She did; scampered up like a mountain goat. She probably hasn't told you because she figures you're a bit too young to be thinking about climbing mountains."

Well, being too young to climb mountains didn't make me too young to *think* about it. In spite of my convictions, I put the idea of mountain climbing to rest until some future date and turned my thoughts to the more imminent subject of the day. School.

In the fall of 1959, the twins and I trotted off to Public School #422 to start our formal education in a first grade classroom. We remained a strongly bonded trio, but even so, before a week had passed, we were reaching out and getting on common footing with other kids in the class. I loved the way Mrs. Hanson challenged our intellect and opened doors to expose cracks of light that shined on doors yet unopened. I felt that I was finally in my element.

Another milestone event took place that fall. David reached the age of thirteen in October. I watched carefully for his reaction when he opened the box containing a new Remington automatic rifle that he got for his birthday.

"I'm asking you to uphold the tradition of the Mowkatah Tribe for my sake, your grandfather's sake, and for the sake of future generations," Dad told him. "When the time comes, David, make me proud; earn your rite of passage into manhood."

I recall the moment as clearly as if it were yesterday. David puffed out his chest and got this look of lust in his eyes as though he could hardly wait for the coming year to go by. I knew then that he'd heard the drum beat and had caught the fever. Yes, I thought, David will live up to his heritage.

Chapter XIV

DAVID TURNS FOURTEEN

As custom demanded, David had a year or so to prepare for the hunt. In the fall of 1960, at dawn on the appointed day, Dad piled David, Uncle Mark, and Cousin Daniel into his station wagon and off they went to a wooded area known to shelter wild white-tailed deer, boar and turkey.

To be brief, about three hundred yards into the forest, David sighted a wild boar foraging for tender morsels of vegetation. He shouldered his rifle, got a bead on the animal and pulled the trigger just as it was about to dive into underbrush. As much as he wanted to shout out loud and dance for joy, he maintained a sober profile, for Mowkatah warriors do not celebrate a kill. Without a moment's hesitation, he went to make sure the animal was indeed dead to preclude prolonged suffering. Then he bowed his head and thanked the animal for giving its life to benefit man. Thus, even though David earned his rite of passage into manhood at the age of fourteen as required by Mowkatah Indian tradition, the animal was considered the star.

Seeing wild game brought home and cut up for the freezer was nothing new at our house and I hadn't really thought about it seriously until David was pressed into going on the hunt. Someday in the future, I, too, would be called upon to perform this ritualistic custom. The idea depressed me and rebellion began to rage within me against the practice even then.

For a year thought of the "hunt" dimmed. Then, when Michael turned thirteen and received a rifle for his birthday, it came to the forefront of my mind again. Seeing him march up the road to the stack of baled hay at the rear of the Campbell farm carrying his rifle to train for the actual event made my stomach turn. I never went to watch him shoot, but I heard through whispers and mumbles that his mark was way off the target.

In fact, on the day of his acid test, he accidently shot a buzzard out of a tree and burned a box of bullets before he managed to bag a couple of wild turkeys; or so the story went. Still, the turkeys earned him the rite of passage into manhood and that's the only thing that seemed to matter.

By then, the twins and I had come to know the town and its environs the way street-smart city kids know the back alleys and sidewalks of their particular turf. The paths leading to the school playground, frog ponds, and swimming holes were kept foot-worn with the help of our padding feet. We knew every inch of the river's embankment from County Road 97 to the spot where it gushed through the break in the base of the ridge. The horses and cows on the Campbell farm knew me by sight and I called them by name.

On more adventurous days, the three of us rode our bicycles further afield and stayed away from home longer. In minutes, we could skirt around the newly dammed lake and slip onto a bicycle trail in the State Park without detection. We had no idea that we were doing anything wrong.

Every now and then at the close of day when I was supposed to be sleeping I would slip out of bed and, with the aid of a flashlight, creep up the stairs to find my way to the north window in the attic. The mountain peaks appeared dark and sinister under moon glow. Drifting clouds drove hordes of eerie shadows over the scene while ghostly fingers of fog played on silent keyboards in mountain hollows. Finally, I figured out that day and night are merely the positive and negative aspects of the same thing. A facet of me craved to know more and more about the mountains; or at least, get a look at them from the top of the mesa.

I decided that the laundry room was as good a place as any for a boy to discuss what ails him with his mother. While Mom folded freshly laundered clothing, I relaxed against a counter, crossed my legs, folded my arms over my chest, and looked on, trying my best to appear nonchalant. The mountains had been so on my mind that I'd hurried home from school to tell her about an idea I had. Happily, I found her in a mellow mood. Good. Now all I had to do was state my case in the right tone of voice; sort of whiny, but not too whiny.

"Mom, it's not my fault George Clawson died of a heart attack and now Grandpa Hollister is too busy making googly eyes at Edna to take me to the top of the mesa like he promised. Anyhow, why can't I go by myself? You and Dad said I could when I turned nine, so why can't I, Mom, huh?"

"You're not nine yet, Billy. Besides, I don't think grandpa has forgotten your birthday at all. He'll take you and show you my old hide-away."

"You had a hide-away on the mesa? a secret place?"

"Yes, the only person I ever took there was your daddy. Even your grandpa didn't know about it until recently. I'm sharing it with you because I think you'll appreciate it. It's part of my birthday gift to you. When you need to be quiet and contemplative, it's a wonderful place to be."

Green eyes brimming with emotion, I went and pulled her face to mine and kissed her lightly on the lips, and then I backed away and put my fingertips together to describe a sphere. "Mom, the air inside of this pretend ball is like your gift to me; you can't taste it, feel it, touch it, see it, or smell it. It didn't cost anything; what do you suppose it is?"

Mom's laughter rang out at my silly antics. "Billy, are you playing games; or are you telling me that I'm giving you a lot of nothing?"

A tight little frown screwed up my face. "No, don't you see? Your gift is sheer magic; it's there, but you can't behold it." For a moment I had forgotten the plan I'd come in with. "Mom, I was thinking that if Grandpa Hollister can't take me and you won't let me go alone, maybe Grandpa Briarwood will make the climb with me."

"I'm sure Grandpa Briarwood would love to go with you, Billy, but he doesn't know the trails. Also, he has arthritic knees. It would be painful for him."

"Well then, why don't we call Grandpa Hollister up and remind him in case he did forget."

"Billy, sometimes you exasperate me. There's a package from your grandfather in the cubbyhole under the stairwell; take it out and open it. Maybe it'll give you a clue. I didn't want to give it to you just now, but...."

When I opened the box and saw that it contained hiking boots, I was ecstatic. Eagerly, I went and sat on a straight-back chair, took off my tennis shoes and tried on the boots. They were a perfect fit.

"He's going to take you on a climb Saturday so he can be here to celebrate your birthday with the family on Sunday. He'll be bringing Edna with him; won't that be nice?"

"I guess so," I said, loving everyone in the world at the moment. "This is going to be my best birthday ever."

"You've many years ahead of you my darling son; I hope you will celebrate scores of birthdays every bit as rewarding."

Chapter XV

BILLY CLIMBS KEBOR'S MESA

The sun had just breached the horizon in the eastern sky, transforming a residue of snow and ice into glistening jewels when Grandpa and I departed 117 Nutmeg Lane. The air was cool and crisp, our breathing left traces of vapor, and the path was littered with fallen leaves. Grandpa carried a knapsack which I didn't think was necessary since we were only going to take a look at the mountains and come home again, but as it happened one of the items he carried was essential to the success of this particular trip.

"All right now, Scamp, the trail behind the Campbell farm is the easiest; we can take it or we can take the west trail which is, hmm...., well, I'll say a little more challenging to your legs. I wouldn't advise attempting any of the others until you get better acquainted with the mesa. Your choice, which way do we go?"

The Riddle of Kebor's Mesa

"Let's take the west trail, grandpa, the one near the old oak tree."

"Ah, so you've been scouting around have you? That tree has been a landmark in that fallow field for as long as I can remember. Some day someone is going to build on the field and then we'll have to find another way to access the west trail; or rather you will, Scamp, because this could be my very last trip."

As we neared the old oak tree the framework of homes under construction could be seen in the woodland on the opposite side of a new chain-link fence. "No Trespassing" signs were posted at specific intervals.

I nodded in that direction. "How do you like the new houses Dad and Mr. Pomeroy are building, Grandpa? The first ten houses sold before they were finished; now they are building fifteen more. Dad is going to build a house high on the slope for us someday. I hope it won't be too soon as I'm not keen about moving. I like our house on Nutmeg."

"Your dad promised your mother when they married that he would build a beautiful home for her some day. He wants to keep that promise. He's a remarkable man, you should be proud of him. I know your grandma would have been."

"Sarah…..? Grandma Hollister?"

"Yes, God rest her soul." His blue eyes glazed over in remembrance. "She would have loved you, Scamp. You have her fair complexion - red hair, green eyes…." He hesitated as his approving look swept over my dark green jacket and brown serge pants; legs tucked into the tops of my hiking boots the likes of which I'd thanked him for a dozen times over. "Yes," he repeated softly, "she would have loved you."

As we continued to ascend the gentle grade of the hill, I noticed that the stout branches of the old oak tree had splintered since my last visit and the bole showed signs of internal decay. The tree is returning to the earth, I thought, and then I noticed the three saplings growing at its base, and smiled.

Grandpa paused beside me and, with hand to chin, studied the trail ahead. Left undisturbed, it had become all but obliterated by smothering vegetation. "Are you afraid to go into that jungle,

Scamp? It's as black as night and it will take a few minutes before we see daylight again."

With Grandpa at my side, I had no demons to fear. "Well then Grandpa, the sooner we get started, the sooner we'll get through it," I said and laughed lightheartedly; my spirits rising to the occasion.

Once we were inside the forest we hiked single file; Grandpa leading the way along a narrow trough where Rocky Ridge met the base of Kebor's Mesa. As he wielded his machete on low-hanging branches, he nimbly dodged thick brush and stepped over tree roots. The air was cold, the forest claustrophobic, the path rugged, and visibility limited, making each minute seem like ten. At an outcropping shaped like a half-buried beehive, grandpa sheathed the machete and returned it to the knapsack. Then with the force of his weight he pushed through a mass of low-growing shrubbery into a clearing where vegetation was sparse and the passage ahead was plainly visible.

Hiking side by side now, conversation came easier. "Dad says Kebor's Mesa is a mystery because mesas are normally found out west and not around here," I remarked.

"That's true, and there are a number of odd-shaped sedimentary rock formations on the summit that are peculiar to the mesa. It's something for people to wonder about, nothing more," he commented and shook his head. "Of course, the white shards are impossible to explain; you'll see for yourself when we get to them."

Cautiously and methodically we followed a winding trail to the summit. A couple of fox holes and hillside caves excited my imagination as we passed them by. About midway, we stopped at a high-bush cranberry shrub and munched on the berries that had survived the winter. On top of the mesa, Grandpa pointed out a large stand of virgin timber and an eagle's nest built high in the branches of a yellow birch tree, a tree rarely seen in the region. The sight of a herd of deer taken unaware held me in awe.

"There should be a big red rock around here somewhere; watch for it on the left of the trail," Grandpa said.

We hadn't gone far when I spotted it. "Is that it, Grandpa...., there, the big red rock next to the fir tree?"

"I don't know how you saw it, Scamp, it's almost completely covered with vines, but this has to be it. We'll know for sure in a minute," Grandpa replied. He removed a flashlight from his knapsack and placed the knapsack on the ground. Beckoning me to follow, he went around to the rock's northern exposure, pulled clinging vines away and showed me where shards of white stones were embedded about chest high in the surface of the rock. All of the stones were either square or oblong in shape. They ranged in size from one to three inches and were spaced at odd angles an inch or so apart. I counted eleven of them.

"In the shade they don't merit a second glance, but watch what happens when they're under a beam of light," Grandpa said. Focusing the flashlight on the shards caused them to light up with pinpoints of brightness that rivaled the stars.

"Gosh! Grandpa, the stones sparkle just like...., just like the beads in my cricket box," I exclaimed. Excitedly, I extracted the cricket box from my pocket and slid the lid back to reveal the contents – three crystal beads and seven silver dimes.

Grandpa was amazed when he saw the crystal beads. "Where did you get those, Scamp?"

"I found them in the attic a long time ago. I thought they were marbles. Mom said I could keep them," I answered, and held one of them up to the sun. "See how the sunlight radiates from it; the same as with the stones."

"Those beads are the same as the ones in the crystal chandelier hanging in the dining room at home. I am touched to see that you keep your small treasures in the cricket box I made for you."

"The beads are my good luck charms. I got the silver dimes from Aunt Minnie so they mean a lot to me, too. I keep them in the box so they don't get separated." What I didn't tell Grandpa was that I held the beads in my hand when I meditated, and for the comfort they elicited when I felt troubled.

"It's possible that the stones in this rock contain specks of crystal, but who knows for sure?

These are the only ones I've seen, but then I've never taken the time to look for more. The arrangement of the stones could easily be construed as the handiwork of an intelligent being, but that notion is too far-fetched to let fester. As curious as I am about them, I prefer to think of them merely as a fluke of nature and let it go at that. Our destination is close Scamp, so let's go take a look at those mountains," he said and reached for the knapsack.

The north rim of the mesa offered a wide variety of vantage points where earth-bound creatures might go to feast on the splendiferous view of the mountains and soar in fantasy to faraway places. Grandpa steered me to a sedimentary rock formation that was also unique to the region. Firmly anchored to the mesa, the pyramidal formation was reminiscent of a huge stack of odd sized pancakes that had been doused with a coating of syrup and then had solidified, transforming the many layers into a single unit. A nearby stand of stately loblolly pines provided shade at certain hours of the day, but not at the moment. By now, we were both beginning to flag and a shelf-like protuberance near ground level appeared very inviting.

"This is probably the most popular lookout on the mesa. It is where I always came to enjoy the scenery," Grandpa told me, and then he stretched his neck to look around as though expecting company. "Seldom did I have it to myself; it was a rare day when no one else was here. However, it is not the isolated place your mother had in mind. We are going to leave the trail and walk east across that barren field," he said further and pointed.

As we approached the spot Mom referred to as her hide-away we could see nothing enticing about the scene, but rather a place one would normally steer away from. This specific section of the mesa had a precipitous edge. The trees in the area displayed only the upper branches, indicating that their roots were buried in earth forty or fifty feet below the summit. There was nothing to suggest that a broad rock ledge extended from the side of the mesa just six feet or so below the rim. Thus, it was understandable why the hidden haven had received no special interest throughout the years.

When Grandpa and I discovered the ledge we laughed, and without further deliberation, clambered over the side of the mesa. Grandpa emitted a satisfied "A-ah," as he lowered his weight to the smooth stone that seemed to have been carved by time and the elements specifically for the comfort of the human frame. Sighing with sheer pleasure, I sat beside him and let my body go limp, but only after I'd seen that we had an excellent view of the mountains.

High above the valley town of Redbud, Grandpa delighted in the same scene he had witnessed a hundred times before. Being unfamiliar with the wide-lens view, I could but stare, fascinated beyond belief.

Ancient as mountains go, the Smokey's dome-like crowns with their gentle slopes melted into the winter sky and became lost in the haze on the far horizon. Seemingly, they went on forever. Nearer to us, I could distinguish rocky features through the lacy branches of a leafless forest. Soon those details would be veiled again by the burgeoning of spring. A meandering river scored the floor of the narrow valley below and strung together a series of small cigar-shaped lakes. On the far side of the river a dirt road led to a couple of weathered shacks. The road and shacks were the only visible evidence of man's assault on the land.

As though all else were window dressing and Mount Angel Head were the grand prize, my eyes returned again and again to the one peak set apart by its tremendous size. Rising above its sister peaks in the near distance Mount Angel Head personified might and majesty.

The sky was clear, so Mount Angel Head wore no halo of clouds, but she did wear a crown of snow that melted as the minutes ticked by. The dark greens of firs and pines mingling with the grays and browns of bare trees contrasted with the deep blue sky. Although the scene lacked the vivacious colors of autumn, it still had the power to dazzle such as me.

Grandpa broke the silence. "It's time we got back down. I've got a date with a young lady this evening and I'm going to want to take a nap."

"Oh, Grandpa, Miss Edna is not young."

"Sixty-one looks mighty young when you're sixty-eight, Scamp."

Chapter XVI

BILLY'S NINTH BIRTHDAY

Birthdays were always celebrated by my immediate family, but not always in a conventional way. My ninth birthday happened to fall on the same Sunday my parents were planning a dinner party to entertain guests. To simplify matters, they planned to celebrate my birthday when dinner was over; serving my birthday cake with coffee for dessert.

Grandpa and Grandma Briarwood arrived well ahead of the five o'clock dinner hour, carrying a Shoo-fly pie and a gift for me. As always, Grandma Briarwood gave me a smacking kiss on the forehead and a squeeze against her bosom before pulling at my hair playfully. "Happy birthday, sweet William," she said, her smile as broad as her rosy-cheeked face.

"Aw, Grandma, a sweet William is a flower. I'm not a flower."

"You are my fair flower, William, and who is to say you are not sweeter than maple syrup?" Grandma Briarwood was the only one in the family who insisted on calling me by my given name which, somehow, made me feel special.

Throughout the years, Grandpa Briarwood instilled knowledge in me that I would have never learned in a classroom. Like Dad and my brothers, I inherited his zest for nature. He had an encyclopedic mind and at every opportunity shared a nugget of wisdom with me.

"Grandpa, Grandpa, do you have a nugget for me?" I knelt on the floor in front of him, eager for his attention.

Putting his hand to his chin, he lapsed into his thinking mode and mulled over the question. "How about this, Billy, 'Above every dark cloud, the sun shines brightly.'"

"Grandpa, you told me that one before," I protested.

"Ah well now, you're testing my memory Billy, but I do have another one for you: 'Always listen to your heart, Grandson, for your heart does not lie.'"

Isn't it strange how a simple little adage can leave a lasting impression on your mind? This one would serve me well in the years ahead. I was still dwelling on the full meaning of the words when the doorbell sounded; ring, ring, pause, ring, ring.... "It's Grandpa Hollister!" I shouted and ran to the door.

How different they were in physical attributes and attitude, I thought, as Grandpa Hollister came waltzing in, literally bouncing with youthful vitality. He had Edna Clawson on his arm and she, too, was all aglow, done up in a navy blue pant suit; every strand of hair in place. I'd pictured her as an old lady with a pinched face and an aloof air. Say what you like, I was damned if I was going to like her, but how could I help myself? She looked young, and happy, and smiley, and she had those "love me" puppy-dog brown eyes. Shoot! I could see why Grandpa was smitten.

We were grouped on overstuffed furniture in the living room, waiting for the rest of the guests to arrive before Mom put the food on the table so we could eat. Grandpa Hollister chose the moment to announce that he and Edna were to marry in May.

"Maybe it will stop tongues from wagging," he said, "not that it matters; a piece of paper doesn't make a marriage. Anyway, we'll be living in Britt's Bay until I retire in two years. We don't know what we'll do afterward; that bridge will be crossed when we get to it."

At Grandpa's words, I saw Mom go pale and reach for Dad's hand.

So well did they know each other, the gesture conveyed her concern to Dad as clearly as if they had spoken

Evidently, Grandpa also read the message for he elaborated on his statement at once. "One thing is certain, we won't be coming back to live in the valley; we'll be looking at communities that cater to the elderly. So....," he began again and stopped to emit a soft chuckle, "you folks don't have to worry about being evicted."

Mom heaved a sigh and relaxed her head on Dad's shoulder. Body language – it's so easy to decipher when you know the person and the way that person thinks.

The Campbell clan showed up next - old Jed and Nora, Jim and Peggy, and the twins Stephen and Susan - my bosom buddies.

Dinner on my birthday would not have been complete without the presence of Minnie Gibson. She arrived last accompanied by a strange tall man who escorted her into the foyer when I opened the door.

I barely recognized her; she might have been a high stepping model out of Vogue Magazine instead of the bedraggled woman who had fostered me. An orthodontist had done a remarkable job on her teeth. The mousy colored hair I had known was now golden ash in color and "done," I'm sure, by a bona fide beautician. Beneath her stylish clothing, she obviously wore proper undergarments – as opposed to none.

It so happened that when George Clawson died, he left Redbud's Post Office without a Postmaster. As a result, the remaining employees at the office moved up the ladder, leaving a vacancy on the bottom rung. Minnie filled the vacancy as a part timer. Although the job prohibited her from working for Mom on Thursdays, she continued to be a close friend to the family. However, this was my first encounter with her in almost a year.

"Aunt Minnie, you're…. you're looking great," I exclaimed. "It's good to see you after so long a time."

"It's been too long; much too long." She hugged me and then held me away to give me an appraising look from the tips of my shiny brown Oxfords to my unruly red hair. "Oh, my, Billy, you're growing like a weed," she remarked, and then addressed her companion, "Frank, this is the boy I've been telling you about; the one I helped deliver on a rainy day exactly nine years ago. Billy," she went on, turning her attention back to me, "meet my good friend, Frank Carstaires. Soon, I'll be working in his restaurant."

"It's nice to meet you, Mr. Carstaires," I said, frowning. Is your restaurant far from here?"

"Not unless you call the property across from your father's development 'far,'" he said, one dark eyebrow raised in amusement and lips curled into a winning smile under a thin mustache.

"That's good news. When will it open?"

The Riddle of Kebor's Mesa

"You might ask your father or Mr. Pomeroy; they promised to start excavating next week. By the way, Happy Birthday, Billy; I hope you get the presents you want."

"I hope so, too, but what I really want doesn't come in a package."

At that instant, Dad approached. He kissed Minnie on the cheek and offered a hand to Frank. "I'm glad you could join us," he said, and then, "Minnie would you mind introducing Frank to the folks? I'll be with you in a minute; I need to talk to my son."

I never could tell what went on behind Dad's steel gray eyes. Now I wondered if I'd done something to displease him, or said something out of turn. What?

Taking me to one side, Dad placed a hand on my shoulder. The simple gesture made me feel warm and tingly inside. Right then, I wanted to throw my arms around him and declare my profound love for him. I knew he loved me, but for some reason I couldn't fathom the barrier that existed between us; I could get just so close before running into a brick wall. To salve my ego,

I rationalized. Like Mom – who was too busy with the house to give me much of her time - he was probably too busy on the job and teaching my brothers the tricks of the trade to find time to cater to my individual needs. Somehow, the reasoning softened the hurt.

My brothers, David and Michael, were spitting images of Dad, mannequins of masculinity with black shiny hair and good looks – the whole bit - so understandably, they were heralded as "Briarwoods." I, on the other hand, with my red hair, fair skin and freckles, was often referred to as a "Hollister." Is it any wonder that I sometimes felt *apart* from the family and not a *part* of it? All I really wanted was for Dad to verbalize his love for me. Was it so hard to say, "I love you Billy?"

Of course, I couldn't tell Dad how I felt at that very moment. I stood mute, reached into my pocket, thumbed the lid off of the cricket box and began to finger the crystal beads as I waited to hear what he had to say.

"You're getting some pretty nice presents for your birthday Billy; what is it you want that can't be packaged?"

Emboldened by yesterday's successful assault on the mesa, I dared to meet his steady gaze. "I would like to have your and Mom's permission to climb the mesa on my own before the trail grows cold," I replied.

"You must have had a good time with your grandfather," he said, and then straightened and looked into the distance for a lengthy moment before focusing again on his red haired son. I sensed his feeling of guilt and the spark of envy tightening his chest. His inner conflict was evident in his tone of voice. "I'll speak to your mother and grandfather and let you know."

The meal was done to perfection, as usual. Even Grandpa Briarwood, who was of the opinion that no one could match Grandma Briarwood's culinary skills, patted his pot belly and gave Mom a complimentary salute. While biding time for the meal to settle before serving coffee and cake, conversation flowed from one topic to the next - the weather, further elaboration on Joseph and Edna's imminent wedding, Frank's proposed restaurant, the status of Redbud's new subdivision, and David's impending graduation from high school.

"Have you decided what you want to do after you graduate high school, Dave?" Dad asked.

David had been mulling the situation over for weeks, trying to decide whether go to a university and test his skills at alternate vocations or continue to pursue the path he was already on – the field of carpentry. One flaw in the present set-up prevented him from committing himself and that was the fear of spending his entire working life under Dad's jurisdiction; always an underling, never quite an equal.

Like the rest of us in the family, David harbored deep thoughts, laid claim to a personal God, and meditated; none of which had helped him so far. However, at that very instant, the solution hit him squarely on the chin; so simple it made him strike the heel of a hand to his temple and laugh. "Of course!" he cried. Then flashing a smile not unlike Dad's own, he squared his shoulders and spoke with the confidence of a major player on stage; and with an apparent show of arrogance too.

"I know what I want to do, Dad. If you and Mr. Pomeroy agree; I want to work full time through the summer as an apprentice. In the fall

I'll want my hours reduced to give me time to take a course in Constructive Engineering at the Constantine College of Technology in Britt's Bay. With all due respect," he went on, "after I've earned my degree, if you still want me, I'll expect to be recognized as a full-fledged partner. I'll want to work *with* you and Mr. Pomeroy, not *for* you."

As dad listened to his eldest son's plans for the future, he swore he felt the earth quake, he was so proud. "Your decision pleases me very much," he said, and then in a bid to include Michael in the discussion, he said to his second son, "You're blessed with many talents Mike; have you any idea what course you might want to take when you finish high school?"

"I think I could be happy working as a carpenter if I didn't find math so easy. Anyway, I still have two years to figure it out," Michael answered.

"When the time comes, I hope you'll follow your brother's example, but the decision will be yours to make," Dad said. Then, "Now if no one objects, Kathy and I will clean up this mess so we can bring Billy's birthday cake out."

Taking his cue from dad, Grandpa Hollister took the floor. "Speaking of our birthday boy; let me tell you about the climb we made yesterday...."

Grandpa's glowing account of our journey to the mesa convinced Mom and Dad that I was responsible enough to be trusted with such activity. Agreeing to loosen my tethers, they granted me the ultimate birthday wish. From then on I had their permission to frequent the mesa on my own as long the trip didn't interfere with my assigned duties.

For reasons I can't quite understand myself, I preferred going to Kebor's Mesa alone. With the patient steadfastness of a prospector panning for gold, I subsequently scoured every square inch of the summit in search of rocks embedded with shards of flat, white stones. Over a course of months I discovered no more rocks bearing the unusual shards. The mystery remained just that – a mystery; but was it in truth merely a fluke of nature? I wondered.

Like Mom before me, I made the rock ledge my home away from home; a place to view the mountains, to daydream, and to contemplate the mystery of the universe and the God-force that ran it. Even though my thoughts were apt to be profound and seeking, the moment I returned home I was just a kid again; doing homework, riding my bike, watching television, looking for companionship, or, as it happened more often of late, trying to get a baseball game going.

Chapter XVII

BASEBALL AND THE DUGGAN'S

In the summer of 1963, baseball brought a small fragmented group of us together and solidified our sense of allegiance. Stephen and I were already strongly linked; now, mainly because of baseball, Rickey Sullivan, Marvin Purcell, Lenny Schneider, Danny Smith, and a half dozen other boys in the neighborhood were drawn into my circle of friends. Calling our team the Warriors, we competed with the Royal Blues, the Sly Foxes, and the Silver Arrows; the Silver Arrows being our most abrasive rivals.

Undisciplined and disorganized, with only a modest notion as to what the game was all about, we were of the consensus that a baseball, a bat, a couple of mitts, and a place to run bases fulfilled the requirements for a game. If the diamond adjacent to the school grounds happened to be unavailable, we simply took the game to an alternate playing field which, in many instances, meant the field near the old oak tree

All was well in Redbud until the Duggan's moved to town. They moved in on July 5' 1964. I remember the date well because it was the day after Redbud featured a brilliant display of fireworks in the town square for the first time.

They came, Clarence and Sheila Duggan and their son Larry in a rickety van followed by a stake truck heaped high with household furnishings, to occupy the easternmost house on North River Road.

The upscale house, built prior to WWII, was situated on two acres of land directly across from the Campbell farm complex. The Limerick River meandered around the east-end and back of the property as it journeyed forth. In other words, the Duggan's closest neighbors were at least a city block away; perfect for what Clarence intended.

Early one evening a group of us boys and girls gathered around the old oak tree as we often did just for the camaraderie. We were munching on peaches from the orchard and chattering and laughing about nothing in particular when Larry

The Riddle of Kebor's Mesa

came marching across the field with his father following in his wake like an eagle hovering protectively over its only chick.

As they approached, Stephen and I left the others and went to greet them.

"Hi, I'm Larry Duggan and this is my father Clarence; we just moved here from Punkin Hollow. I was wondering…., do you have a baseball club?" He asked.

"I don't know about having a club, but we play baseball. We're the Warriors," I replied.

He glanced at the girls in the group. "Do the girls play on your team?" he asked.

Not in competition," I informed him, "but sometimes they help us practice."

"That's nice of them," he remarked politely, then, "I'd like to belong to your team. I'm a pretty good catcher."

"He's a damn good catcher," Clarence interjected; his voice sounding like the roar from a freight train running out of control.

The Riddle of Kebor's Mesa

"I catch for the team," Stephen informed him. "You're welcome to play, but you'd be a sub until a permanent spot opened up."

"That's okay with me," Larry said, making a clucking sound of appreciation.

"Where's your playing field?" the voice wanted to know.

"This is it," I replied, nodding to the plot of scraggly ground that had the imprint of a much used square on it. "Well, we play on the school diamond, too, when it isn't in use."

"Huh! This is a cow pasture. We just moved out of a hell hole that has a better baseball field than this," Clarence Duggan stated gruffly. He then strode to first base and gave it a kick. "Is this what you call a base? a gunny sack filled with dirt?"

A guess placed Clarence Duggan at about forty-five. Dark thinning hair with a mind of its own fell in bangs on his forehead. Squinty brown eyes peered out from behind tortoise-rimmed glasses. He probably stood five-eleven. While he was not exactly muscular, he was lean and well toned; mindful of a man who is on his feet a lot and watches what he eats.

He grew quiet. Thoughtfully, he hooked his thumbs in his pants pockets and scoped out the new development to his left, raised his head to view Kebor's Mesa, and then slowly panned around, taking in the town's picturesque setting. A minute crept by. Finally, he nodded.

"This town needs a decent baseball field for kids," he said. "Tell you what…., what did you say you call yourselves? Warriors? Tell you what Warriors, you put Larry on your first string of players and you and your teammates will get a baseball diamond you can be proud to play on."

He started away quickly, as though in a huff, then spun around and faced the group once more. Supporting an elbow on one hand, he put the other to his chin. "Who schedules the games and keeps a record of the scores?"

"No one does," I told him.

"Do you have an umpire? Does anyone coach you?"

"Uh, uh, we just play."

The Riddle of Kebor's Mesa

"In other words your game stinks," he remarked harshly and left with Larry on his tail.

Based on the rumors that floated around town, Clarence was a top notch sporting goods salesman working for a major department store in Clarksdale. He and Sheila had saved for the day they could afford to get away from the squalor in Punkin Hollow. Having accomplished that, they were now intent on putting roots down in the little valley town of Redbud. Clarence, the aggressor in the marriage, had arrived with an attitude.

Of course, he was well aware of the fact that he was moving into one of the nicer neighborhoods in town; he'd scratched and crawled to get there. He also knew that he could do whatever he damned well pleased with his property and no one could stop him; at least not legally, since Redbud had no legalized building codes.

Exercising what he believed to be his inalienable rights, he drafted his plans and proceeded accordingly. After the last carton of household goods was unpacked and the house was put in order, he took a two-week vacation from his job in Clarksdale, hired a couple of able-bodied teenagers and, with their help, built the promised baseball field on his newly acquired acreage.

Except for skimming an inch or a foot here and there where necessary, the diamond, pitcher's mound, and dugouts were constructed fairly close to specifications. Regulations called for thirteen feet of turf around the bases; he made it twelve feet, believing no one would notice. However, he did leave dirt where it was supposed to be. Home plate was positioned so that the arc of a batted ball's trajectory was toward the road, eliminating - in theory at least - interference with Jim Campbell's livestock and greenhouse, or the possibility of losing a ball in the river. Several rough hewn benches were arranged behind the backstop for the comfort of potential spectators.

It was just the beginning.

Chapter XVIII

ORGANIZED BASEBALL

The Warriors gladly changed their venue from the old oak tree to Duggan's Diamond, as Clarence called it, but continued to play the game as usual with little, if any, supervision. At the same time, most of Redbud's population deemed the ball park a grand gesture of generosity, benefitting the town's youth. Fathers with sons involved in baseball became interested in Clarence's endeavor. As a result, Clarence had no trouble getting men to oversee the games. Many came forward eager to serve in whatever capacity needed – equipment-handler, scorekeeper, coach, manager, or whatever.

However, among the small percentage of people in the community who were unhappy with Duggan's Diamond were those who raised questions concerning Clarence's true character. Was he really altruistic? Or, had he concocted some devious scheme to take advantage of small town operations? Dad and the Campbell's were undecided.

Even so, believing that I stood to profit from the baseball experience, Dad donated a sum of money to Clarence to be used for incidental expenses. He also provided maroon colored Tee-shirts, emblazoned with the company logo on the backs, for each of the Warriors.

Despite the murmurs of dissent from certain quarters, an organized baseball club, consisting of four teams, opened the 1965 season on a Saturday afternoon in May. By a draw of straws the Silver Arrows and Warriors were the first to play at Duggan's Diamond while the remaining two teams were scheduled to play on the school's diamond.

A fair sized crowd attended Duggan's Diamond partly out of curiosity, no doubt, but mostly to witness the ongoing rivalry between the two most popular teams in town.

Unaccustomed to having grown-men watch every move made, the players tended to be tense and awkward. Errors were made. Surely, we appeared amateurish and a little befuddled. Nevertheless, we put forth a spirited, crowd-pleasing exhibition, trying with all our might to be beat the opposition. Really good plays were rare, but when they happened they brought roars of approval from the sidelines. Stephen leaped up and caught an "impossible-to-catch" fly ball in the second inning. Pete Fulton, pitcher for the Silver Arrows, got a home run in the fourth inning. I got a two-base hit in the fifth and connected for a homer in the seventh.

In spite of the fact that onlookers responded with all of the hoopla and hullabaloo expected at an entertaining ballgame something was missing and Clarence knew exactly what it was.

When the game was over, he wrung his hands gleefully, danced a little jig, and uttered a veiled "Heh, heh!" to himself. The ball park was destined to be a tremendous success; he could feel it in his bones. Why wait to make the next move, he reasoned, when the time was ripe now?

So what if the area was not zoned for commercial use. After all, this was the town of

Redbud; there wasn't a law on the books that said he couldn't vend as long as he had a license.

Consequently, Clarence bought an old house trailer for a song and converted it into a concession stand. He then stocked it with beverages and edibles that were easy to store and had a long shelf life. Viola! He was in business.

Sheila managed the concession stand during his absences, but when he was available he hustled the wares. The amount of money he made on nickel and dime items during a game amazed him. Oh, what a heavenly feeling to be raking it in instead of shelling it out. Wasn't it only right and just that he get back some of the fortune he'd spent on the park? Of course! But then as a newcomer in town, he figured it wise to tread softly; take his time, play the "wait and see" game before expanding his operation further.

When the 1965 and 1966 baseball seasons came and went without incident, Clarence decided it was safe to take his ambitions a step further. During the winter months, he equipped the concession stand with heavy duty appliances capable of dispensing hotdogs, hamburgers, French fries, ice cream bars and coffee. The grills

The Riddle of Kebor's Mesa

were sizzling at Duggan's Diamond when the teams assembled to begin the 1967 season.

Two years can make a definitive difference in anybody's journal. At Duggan's the crowds were bigger and sales multiplied accordingly. The players had become well versed with the mechanics of the game; they understood the rules, played with greater finesse, had tougher muscles, and hit the ball farther. In late August, a player hit a baseball into the ditch on the far side of the road, alerting Clarence to the possibility of trouble.

He immediately erected a ten-foot high wire-mesh fence along the front of his property without concern for its appearance, or how it affected the aesthetics in the neighborhood. Residents living on North River Road resented the fence. They took pride in their sprawling ranch type homes, manicured lawns, and fancy greenery. The ball park had already depreciated the value of the property; and now, that ugly fence!

The Campbells, too, were beginning to worry about conditions at the ball park; especially after finding several baseballs lying in the grass inside their fence line. However, when no one confronted Clarence Duggan, he labored under the impression that the ballpark had become a permanent and appreciated fixture in town; that it was accepted and embraced by all who flocked to the games regularly. Meanwhile, he was making more money than he knew what to do with.

Building upon the foundation of his original idea, he brazenly installed flood lights around the perimeter of the ball park in readiness for the 1968 season. He also replaced the benches behind the backdrop with three-tier bleachers.

The flood lights made it clear to the people of Redbud that Clarence planned to schedule night games and extend the playing season. In a less apparent maneuver, he advertised the availability of time slots at Duggan's Diamond for the upcoming baseball season in all of the nearby towns — Clarksdale, Plighton, Fenton, Punkin' Hollow, Benev, and Willowford.

Yes, I was looking forward to playing baseball in the spring. I had cultivated the ability to hit the longest ball of anyone playing on the charter teams. I had a knack for out-guessing the pitchers on opposing teams and seldom struck at a foul pitch. However, neither baseball nor Kebor's Mesa occupied my thoughts on Saturday, February 10, 1968; the day I turned fourteen.

It has been told before, but bears repeating; predicated by a tradition that persisted through untold generations, fourteen was the age at which young males in the Briarwood family were initiated into the sport of hunting. Dad's inducement had assured David and Michael's adherence to the legacy; now it was my turn. I had attained that critical period in life when the boy in me was supposed to yield to some macho mechanism in my genes and turn me into a man.

Chapter XIX

THE BEGINNING OF A TOUGH YEAR

Aunt Minnie was now Mrs. Carstaires. Together she and Frank proudly ran the only upscale restaurant in Redbud. They had named it simply, "Food Unleashed." The family plus David's fiancée, Arlene, helped me celebrate my fourteenth birthday in those posh surroundings. The occasion called for finery; the men in suits, ties and polished shoes; the ladies in dressy dresses, appropriate accessories and smart hairdos.

No matter how many times I attended the place – and the family went there often – I couldn't help but swell with pride knowing Dad had designed every detail of the building.

Patterned after a Swiss chalet, he had used colorful chiseled stone on the base of the exterior to support sheet-size windows framed in broad vertical planks of weathered wood that had been stained dark green. Slate shingles covered the kingpost type roof of the main building then sloped gently over a ballroom annex. Landscaping, made up of green grass, evergreen shrubs and tall, slender fir trees, completed the exterior image. The interior, from the beamed ceiling to the carpeted floor, radiated a warm and alluring ambience. Gleaming leather was used extensively; aqua in the booths along the outside walls and dark green on the arm chairs at the tables in the main dining area. Soft lighting glowed from elegant chandeliers. Tall, healthy indoor plants, growing in massive pieces of crockery, were placed about the large room and in each of the side rooms. A highly polished mahogany bar stretched across the rear of the building, allowing space for access to the men's and women's restrooms on either side. Customers could sit on cushioned stools at the bar, sip drinks and watch food being prepared in the brick-lined kitchen at the far end. Everything had its own specific appeal, even the aroma and the light-as-a-breeze music filtering from the annex.

Minnie seated us in the privacy of one of the side rooms and personally served us a lavish meal, making certain the menu included my favorite recipe for chicken and dumplings. Following the meal and the cake-and-candle ritual, dad and mom carried my presents and cards in and placed them on the table, some of which were from people not in attendance. One by one I opened them, noting with profound appreciation the fielder's mitt from David and Arlene, the new baseball from Michael, and the instamatic camera from Aunt Minnie and the man I now called Uncle Frank. To my dismay, I found nothing among the gifts from my parents.

Unable to account for the oversight, I wondered if I had overlooked a cash gift in an envelope, but then I met Dad's amused look and watched as an infectious smile spread across his handsome face, revealing to me that my parents had indeed a gift for me; one that couldn't be opened in the restaurant. My stomach knotted as I pictured the dreaded gun! What else could it be?

"We have something for you at home Billy; we'll give it to you there," he said, exuding the warmth and affection that I so cherished.

A short time later, David, Arlene and Michael were on their way to Britt's Bay in David's car to keep an appointment with a group of mutual friends; while I sat across from Mom and Dad in the living room of our house, staring at a long, narrow carton lying on top of the coffee table between us.

"You've just turned fourteen Billy, so I think you know what's in the box," Dad said.

"Yes, I do, Dad," I replied, instantly realizing that the flat, unenthusiastic response revealed my true sentiments. I had unintentionally rebuffed my parents' gift and may have hurt their feelings. I hung my head, crestfallen.

"You've made it clear for some time now that you are not exactly keen about going on the hunt this fall, but we bought a gun for you anyway," Dad said and paused, before quickly adding, "for a good reason." The timbre of his voice begged understanding.

"Billy, look at me," Mom said and waited for me to raise my head and meet her eyes. "I'm going to leave you to hash this out with your father. Listen to what he has to say. It grieves me to see you so squeamish about killing something you relish putting a fork into." With that statement, she rose and kissed Dad. "I'll be upstairs, Hon," she said, and coming to me, kissed my cheek and whispered, "Think of what this means to your father, Billy." Exiting at an unhurried gait, she did not look back.

"I want to please you, Dad, but I can't help the way I feel."

"That's what I want to talk to you about, Billy. You see, I grew up loving fishing and hunting; the two sports came natural to me. Then I served in World War II. When I got out of the Army I didn't care if I never saw a gun for the rest of my life. Your Grandfather Briarwood convinced me to try again. He wanted me to regain the zest I lost during the battle overseas. I listened to what he said. I hunted with him and your Uncle Mark the next open season and learned to love the sport again. That's all I'm asking of you, son; give it a try. I'd hate for you to be the one in the family to break tradition," he explained tolerantly.

"Why are traditions so important?"

"Traditions define us; they are part of who we are. Without them we'd all be stereotypes," Dad answered, his patience growing thin.

"What are stereotypes, Dad?"

"Damn it, Billy, no more questions; just try to think like a Briarwood for once. Open the carton and take a look at your new rifle. You might as well get a feel for it because you are not going to weasel out this fall and disgrace me and your brothers...., and your grandfather. You will be going on the hunt. You'd better be ready to hit a target."

I felt a jabbing pain at his sudden outburst. I cringed inside and for the first time that I could remember I wanted to pull away from him. Instead of giving in to self-pity, I rose above the hurt with youthful resilience and vowed to make a concentrated effort to live up to his expectations.

Stretching to stand as tall as I possibly could, I reached for the carton, opened it, and withdrew the rifle - a Remington automatic with a telescopic viewfinder. I caressed the smooth patina on the walnut handle, ran my fingers down the length of the gleaming blue barrel, placed it snug against my shoulder and peered through the viewfinder. With mixed emotions I placed the gun back in the carton and tucked the carton under my arm.

"It's a beautiful piece of workmanship. I shouldn't have any trouble hitting a target with this weapon. I promise you Dad, I'll be a marksman by fall," I stated solemnly, and made a move to leave.

"Wait, there's one more thing. Did you know Clarence Duggan is scheduling baseball teams from out of town to play at his facility this spring?"

"No! Why would he do that? I thought the lights were for the charter teams."

"As long as he gets away with it, he'll continue to create problems until something bad happens. I don't want you involved Billy. Promise you won't play there when the season begins."

"Dad, we're already scheduled to play half of our games at Duggan's. I'm part of a team; please don't ask me to let my teammates down."

The room went silent for an awkward moment. Dad ran his fingers through his hair and studied the rebellious gaze in my eyes; bright with unshed tears. Strangely, he suddenly seemed to see something in me he had not recognized before. His features softened and I wondered if he regretted the insensitive remark he'd made. Unfortunately, he could not take it back and an apology would only make matters worse. So why was he pouring salt on the wound? Dear God, I thought, what is going on here?

"No, I'm not going to ask you to do that," he said finally in a voice filled with compassion." You are not responsible for Clarence's actions. However, the first time there is an incident involving Duggan's Diamond, I will not allow you to play there anymore. It's a matter of principle."

"Yes sir, that sounds fair," I said, and changed the subject. "I'm going to need some blank shots, Dad."

During that same period, as a member of the eighth grade student body, I was introduced to social dancing. Over and over again, the students performed to the cadence of the fox trot, repeating the words, "step-together-step," "step-together-step," and to that of the waltz, "ONE, two, three, four," "ONE-two, three, four."

In the beginning, I had little control over my feet. I stepped on toes and was unable to coordinate my movements with those of my partner and still keep time to the music. After several weeks of rehearsal the beat of the music began to seep into the marrow of my bones. My whole body heard the melodious sounds and I pivoted, whirled, and glided in moves I didn't know I had in me; particularly when I danced with Susan. Like father, like son, Mom observed at David and Arlene's wedding.

The double-ring ceremony took place at St. Bartholomew's Presbyterian Church on a sunny Saturday, April 20, 1968 midst ringing church bells, mock-orange blossoms and flickering candles. Never was Arlene more radiant. The lines of her eggshell satin gown were becomingly simple with long sleeves and an overlay of Chantilly lace. Sequins embellished the bodice and the tiara on her finger-tip veil. David beamed with happiness in an off-white tuxedo and a cummerbund borrowed from the material in Arlene's gown.

Michael, serving as best man, was paired with Arlene's best friend, Ocona Miller who wore lavender. Arlene's two brothers and I served as ushers and wore formal attire in a deep shade of ecru and the bridesmaids complimented them in pale green gowns.

At a festive reception dinner in Plighton, families and friends toasted the bride and groom and reveled until late evening. Feeling quite grown up, I danced at least once with the ladies I knew well and saved the rest of the dances for Susan.

When you live in the mountains, you don't honeymoon in them, you go to the shores of some remote place. Dave and Arlene flew to the Bahamas.

The wedding was a nice diversion; it took my mind off of the rifle and bullets for a short spell; but then it was back to target practice again.

Demonstrating patience and concern, Dad coached me on the proper use and care of the gun. Repeatedly, he stressed the safety measures to follow. When he decided that I was ready, he took me to the same stack of baled hay on Jed's farm that my brothers had practiced on when they were getting ready to go on the hunt. He made sure the hay was dense enough to stop a rifle bullet. The new canvas draped over it was, of course, painted with a sizable bull's eye.

In order to get through the ordeal I'd been saddled with, I pretended the gun was a toy – not a lethal weapon; target practice on inanimate objects was a game of make-believe – not a prerequisite for slaughtering game.

Mean while, I vigorously pursued the game of baseball on the school grounds and at Duggan's Diamond; a ball park that had over reached its potential.

With the addition of flood lights and bleachers the tempo around the ball park intensified and the nuisance factor rose to an all-time high. Older, aggressive out-of-town teams and their avid followers came to Redbud in cars, vans, pick-up trucks, and on motorcycles. They were a noisy bunch that parked their vehicles haphazardly on the shoulders of North River Road and littered the grounds with empty beer bottles, tin cans, and food wrappings. They contended for the limited seats in the bleachers and doubled the length of the lines at the concession stand.

At the end of each game Clarence counted the money in his till and did double-entry bookkeeping. Apparently oblivious to the possible fallout of his actions, he also failed to see that the tight fit of his ball park in its surroundings was now showing signs of stress. Instead, he congratulated himself on the ingenuity that had transformed a patch of land into a cash cow with low overhead and no one to keep tabs on his profits.

Playing ball at Duggan's Diamond became a sort of breath-holding affair. The players got into the habit of tracing a high-flying ball to see where it landed and then quickly send someone to retrieve it; grateful that it hadn't broken a window or hit a grazing animal. The inevitable occurred on a Wednesday afternoon near the end of August.

The Warriors were playing against the Sly Foxes and I was up to bat. I knew the pitcher and had figured him out. Slipping under a sinker I hit the ball square on and sent it sailing up, up and away, over Duggan's high wire fence right for the greenhouse.

The round of cheers from the crowd swiftly shifted into a series of groans at the sound of broken glass. I counted myself among the groaners. After running the round of bases, I huddled with the twins.

Stephen gave me a slap on the back, a little harder than necessary, I thought. "Thanks friend, you just created an incident; now I won't be allowed to play here anymore," he said.

Gears grinding, I shot him a glance. "You too?" I asked. "Why do I have the notion that your father and mine have been putting their heads together? Great! Now the manager and assistant manager are off limits at Duggan's. What are we supposed to do?"

Susan gave me a poke. "Don't look now, but here comes Larry with you know who."

Swinging his arms ape-style, Clarence bore down on us with his son scurrying along at his heels. Eyes as hard and black as anthracite, he addressed me, wagging an accusing finger,

The Riddle of Kebor's Mesa

"You're responsible for the broken glass, Billy Briarwood. Do you have the money to pay for it?"

Another time, another place and the raucous, ill-tempered voice might have intimidated me. At the moment I was in no mood for the likes of Clarence Duggan. Ignoring the father, I spoke to the son. "I'll be playing on the school grounds, but I won't be playing here anymore after today. It's nothing personal against you, Larry. In fact, you can act as manager when the Warriors play here." The statement, short and to the point, caused Clarence's jaw to drop.

"What about the glass? Who is going to pay for it?" he asked agitatedly, although I felt sure there was a lot more than the cost of the window on his mind.

"I'll talk to Mr. Campbell and take it from there," I answered.

There was no way out of it other than to face the music; the sooner the better. Of course, having the moral support of the twins when I went to talk to their elders about the matter, gave me a measure of comfort.

The large double doors at the far end of the barn were wide open. A shaft of sunshine highlighted the dust in the air. Some horse riggings and farm tools hung on the walls; others were strewn about. The pungent smell of hay and animal excrements wafted on a light breeze. I was used to the odor and found it inoffensive. Pensively, the three of us made our way toward their father who was seen in silhouette working under the hood of a Diesel-engine tractor with caterpillar treads. He wore bib overalls without a shirt, exposing sun-bleached hair on his back and massive shoulders. He'd mellowed over the years, becoming more relaxed; more talkative.

"Well, well, well, if it isn't my favorite threesome; I don't suppose you're looking for this?" he said, and straightening, he removed a baseball from his pocket. "Now, I wonder who could have broken a window in the greenhouse. I know it wasn't you Susan, so who could it be? Surely not you Steve, or you Bill…."

Raising my hand, I stepped forward. "I'm sorry, Mr. Campbell, I work at the restaurant for Aunt Minnie on Saturday mornings so I'll be able to pay for it; I just haven't got any money on me right now." As I spoke I worried the crystal beads in my pocket with one hand and stroked a magnificent sorrel sire named "Senator" through the slatted gate of its stall with the other. Baring its teeth, it stretched to feel the touch of my hand. "No apples today, boy," I told the horse, and then carried on with Jim. "I guess I won't be playing at Duggan's anymore."

"No, and neither will Steve. Looking at your pitiful faces, I'm inclined to tell you to go ahead and play; but I won't, simply because I'd be a sorry ass father if I did. Clarence Duggan has turned the ball park into a three-ring circus. Your father and I are not punishing you; we are trying to teach you to be responsible for your actions. Just so you know, there is a movement going on behind the scenes to make things right. Please, trust us and be patient, young people."

There is no accounting for feelings, when they are right, you just know it; nobody has to tell you. Perhaps it has to do with vibrations or something. Anyway, ever since my birthday and our discussion about going on the hunt, Dad seemed more charitable toward me; more disposed to accepting me as the person I am. For that reason I had dared to play just one more game at Duggan's.

A day later when dinner was over, I sat at the kitchen table using a crossword puzzle magazine as a prop while I did a brown study over the situation I had created for myself. All I could hear was the tick of the clock and the creaks and groans of the big house caused by the falling temperature outdoors. Dad sat across from me, drinking coffee and reading Britt's Bay's daily newspaper. Without a doubt, he already knew about the broken glass, but should I confess that I'd played in a game against his wishes? Or, carry the burden of the sin to the grave with me?

"By the way," he began casually as he turned a page and searched for a title of interest, "I've never know you to lie, Billy; you've always been straight with me."

I saw the punch coming at once and beat him to it. "Gee, thanks Dad, coming from you that is high praise. I'm glad you mentioned it because there's something I need to tell you."

"Oh, and what might that be?"

"I tagged a ball at Duggan's the other day and busted a window in the Campbell's greenhouse," I said, imparting as impassive an air as well as J knew how.

Settling back in his chair, Dad put the newspaper down, locked his hands behind his head, and gave me one of his unreadable looks. "Did you speak to Jim or Jed about it?"

"Yes sir, I spoke to Jim right away. I offered to pay for the damage, but he said Mr. Duggan was obligated to pay."

"Why didn't you tell me about this sooner?" he wanted to know.

Hesitating uncomfortably, I began to wilt under his steady gaze. "I would have, but...., but the truth is I...., I....,"

"That's what I want from you Billy – the truth."

"Well, the Warriors played against the Silver Arrows yesterday at Duggan's. The team needed me to pitch and Steve to catch. We really make a good battery, Dad, but we didn't bat. Ricky Sullivan pinch hit for me and somebody – I don't

The Riddle of Kebor's Mesa

know who – pinch hit for Steve. That's it, we're not about to play there again," I stated decisively.

Twisting away, Dad scratched his head and stifled a laugh. The face he turned back to me was stone-cold sober and inscrutable. Then, in the wink of an eye, his mood changed again. Arching a brow, he grimaced and considered me fleetingly with pain-filled eyes. Stubbornly resisting a display of emotion, he pushed away from the table. "Let's take a walk, shall we?" he suggested kindly.

"Where do you want to go?" I asked anxiously.

"We'll go anyplace you want to go."

"Let's climb the mesa; we never did that together."

"I've no special interest in your mesa, Billy; but.... all right, the mesa it is."

The grandfather clock chimed seven as we set out. Matching moods made for pleasant companionship that evening. Dad hadn't made the ascent to the summit for over a decade, but he recalled the trails well. He set the pace, scaling the steep slopes effortlessly and taking long strides on the surface, testing my ability to keep up. The topic of the rock ledge came up.

"On my first climb, your mother took me to the rock ledge. I've had a sentimental attachment to it ever since," he said.

In turn, I confided that I often sat on the rock ledge to meditate and considered it sacred ground. Even so, we agreed to go only as far as the pyramidal rock so we could take advantage of the last hour of daylight.

In comfortable silence, standing side by side, Dad and I watched the setting sun melt red into purple and clothe drifting white clouds in pink and gold. Birds, defining lambent arcs, rode air currents over verdant peaks. As always, the splendor touched my soul. I scanned the horizon and then settled my sights on Mount Angel Head.

"Isn't she beautiful, Dad?"

"Hmm, yes, it is a beautiful scene," Dad replied, and then did the unpredictable. He put an arm around my shoulders, pulled me close, and buried his face in my hair. "And you are a very good son." Upon releasing me, he went and sat on the bench-like protrusion of the rock formation. "Sit with me Billy," he invited. "The hunting season opens in a few weeks. Will you be ready to shoot game?"

"It's all I think about. I love you so much Dad, I don't want to disappoint you, but when I picture myself pulling the trigger on a deer or a boar my insides turn to jelly. I'm praying that when my day comes I'll be able to follow through and do as you ask."

"Would it be easier if you switched from a rifle to a shotgun and we went after…., well, rabbits or squirrels for instance? They're nuisance animals and there are more of them around than we need. Maybe you could handle that for a start."

"Maybe, but I prefer to stay with the rifle, Dad. I know it so well when I use it, it sort of becomes a part of me.

Chapter XX

BILLY GOES HUNTING

My day to go on the hunt arrived on Saturday, October 19, 1968; the first day of Dad's two-week vacation. It was open season on rabbits, squirrels, quail, pheasant, grouse and other small game. Close to the hour of ten, I slipped a light red and black checkered jacket over a sweat shirt and blue jeans, loaded my pockets with bullets, took my gun out of the rack, and set out with the man with whom I stood most in awe.

Conditions were perfect for the avid nimrod. The temperature had dipped below freezing over night and a light frost still glazed the land. The air was crisp and felt invigorating. For Dad's sake, I made an effort to convey a lightness of spirit I did not feel.

"Great weather for great sports," I offered conversationally.

"I hope you're referring to hunting," he said.

"I am; hunting and baseball. The Warriors are playing against the Silver Arrows tonight. It will be the last game of the season."

"Let's just keep our minds on hunting for the moment, shall we?" he said with one of his infectious grins; meant to comfort.

Walking beside Dad, I carried the unloaded rifle with the barrel pointed toward the ground as instructed. At the end of West River Road, we crossed the bridge and climbed over the Campbell's fence. This placed us about a quarter of a mile from home. Ordinarily, if Dad had been hunting with anyone else – David, Michael, Jim Campbell or Grandpa Briarwood – he would have gone to any of a wide range of open fields or woodlands where a variety of small game were known to abound. Because he was hunting with me, a most reluctant novice, he got Jed's permission to hunt along the edge of the forest on the back acreage of the farm where old cornstalks had been left to wither. The spot was rife with wild rabbits.

Once we had gained the hunting area I loaded my gun. Now we moved stealthily. Conversation was held to a minimum. Since it was to be my hunt, I did the shooting while dad flushed rabbits from thickets, briar patches, clumps of tall grass; anyplace a rabbit might be hiding. Every time one of the little creatures scampered across our path, he cried, "Aim!" and "Fire!" I never came close; my shots were high, wide, or short. I must have saved a dozen rabbits' lives that day.

Of course, he became annoyed with me. He clamped his teeth tightly and began to flex his jaw repeatedly. I must confess that I was edgy, or perhaps a little paranoid is a better description. I began to giggle nervously which, believe me, didn't help matters.

Periodically, I stopped to reload the gun. Dad continued to flush rabbits and I continued to miss them. We were at a stalemate. Even though I said I was sorry for every miss, I knew that he knew I was missing my targets deliberately. I also knew that if he could prove himself right, he'd make me pay. Somehow, he'd exact a price for all he'd been through to bring me to that point only to have his efforts thwarted, even though the idea was his and I was the unwilling inductee. Loving him, and desperately wanting to live up to his ideals, I steeled myself to kill the next rabbit I saw.

As if the Goddess of the Hunt would have the last laugh, a cottontail darted across the path in front of me and, in a panic, became entrapped in a stand of cornstalks. Too frightened to move, it remained lodged there, quivering, and awaiting its doom.

Glancing Dad's way, I saw his features soften and his eyes brighten with anticipation. He smiled a crafty smile.

"If you don't get this one Billy, something is wrong with the picture," he said gruffly. He was standing to the right and a little to the rear of me. We both had our guns trained on the same fixed target.

"Now go ahead and shoot; if you miss, I'll kill it. One way or another, this rabbit is dead."

This time I didn't have an alibi or a bluff. With the gun snug against my shoulder, safety catch off, finger on the gun's hammer, I got a bead on the animal's head. As tense as a bowstring and breathing shallow, I stood immobile. A full minute passed. And then another.

"Damn it, Billy, shoot!" Dad commanded sternly.

I was keenly aware of the creature's fear and my power over its fate. I had no stomach for the kill. And yet I knew that it was extremely important to Dad. He didn't want to have to tell the guys at work, his older sons, or his father, that his youngest had failed the rite of passage into manhood. "Drawing the first blood is the hardest part of the hunt," he had stated gravely before starting out. "Once you've leaped that hurdle you're on your way to becoming a hunter; a real man."

Heart beating wildly, I continued to waver. Throughout the months of preparation I convinced myself that I would meet Dad's demands when the time came. Motivated by his persistent prodding, I would follow through for the slaughter and go home bearing game for the larder. Now, I found myself incapable of firing the shot that would end the life of the terrified ball of fur facing me. I couldn't pull the trigger. I couldn't. The tension mounted and became unbearable.

"God damn it Billy, shoot that son-of-a-bitchin' rabbit; shoot the damn thing!" dad shrieked in rage.

I could feel the anger in his voice and responded in kind. The something that had been stewing in me all summer bubbled over. For the moment, the man standing close to me appeared as a stranger; intent upon having me live up to his standards, not mine. So you want me to be a man, Dad? Okay, I'll be a man, I thought. Not in your eyes perhaps; but in my own. Suddenly, in a desperate burst of action, I decided to finalize the agony of the event. Spinning around, I aimed and pulled the trigger again and again and again, spending all of the bullets in the gun harmlessly into the "O" in one of his "No Trespassing" signs.

"I kept my promise, dad, I learned to shoot," I sobbed brokenly. Then, wishing the earth would open up and swallow me; I gripped the empty gun and ran.

When I got home, Mother was in the yard sharing dialogue with our next door neighbor

Emma Verducci, Peggy Campbell's mother. At sight of me, her eyebrows lifted and she gave me a questioning look. My jaws were locked and I couldn't have spoken if I had wanted to. I shook my head, certain that my countenance said it all, and went into the house.

    Feeling angry and utterly demoralized, I hastily cleaned my gun and placed it in the rack, packed a sandwich and some fruit in a brown paper bag, and exited by the front door. According to the grandfather clock the time was 11:20 AM. Purposely avoiding the mesa for fear that someone would come looking for me there; I headed for the nearest lake south of the highway. Passing by the little yellow house Aunt Minnie had once lived in brought a flood of nostalgic memories and I wondered how things could have gone so wrong in so short a time.

    Downcast, I walked along the shores of the placid lake until I came back to where I started. Then, selecting a sheltered spot, I sat with my back against the bole of a tree and stared vacantly at leaves drifting gently to the ground as sad-faced clowns enacted tragic scenes inside my brain. How long I remained spaced out, I do not know. The chill in the air began to reach inside my jacket, reminding me of my mortal status; that, and hunger pangs. I reached into the brown paper bag, took out an apple and bit into it. The sound brought Susan running.

Hands in pockets, pink parka wide open to reveal a white turtleneck sweater and gray slacks, she stood before me with an indignant smile on her rosy, wind-blown features.

"So this is where you are," she exclaimed. "Your mother said you came this way. I've been looking all over for you."

"I didn't think she saw me leave the house," I said, "is something up?"

"You may have heard, there's going to be a dance at Town Hall next Friday night. Steve and I are planning to go; I'd like you to go with us. They're going to have a four-piece, blue-grass band. It will be a lot of fun."

"Why the hurry, the dance is a week away; you could have told me about it in class Monday," I pointed out, and put the core of the apple in the bag and took out the sandwich. "Here, have half; it's minced ham with lettuce and mustard."

"Thanks, I had lunch," she said. "I didn't want to tell you Bill, but the truth is I lied."

"Now we're getting somewhere. The truth is you lied. Would you mind elaborating on that?" I said and bit into the sandwich.

"Pete Fulton asked to take me to the dance. I told him I didn't date and that I was going on my own. He persisted, said that he'd meet me there and we could be partners for the night. I told him you were going to be my partner. I lied, Bill, but he caught me off guard and I didn't know what else to say." Gathering her coat around her, she squirmed into it, giving the impression that she felt at fault for the incident.

At mention of the lumber giant heir's name "Pete Fulton," the green-eyed monster reared its ugly head. Jealousy was a new emotion for me where Susan was concerned and I wasn't prepared to deal with it.

"That lousy bastard, I ought to kick the shit out of him," I declared passionately. "If it's possible, I'll go to the dance, just to keep his filthy hands off you, but I can't promise. I don't know what's going to happen at home."

"What's wrong at home, Bill?" she asked and sat down beside me to listen to my tale of woe.

At every baleful detail she commiserated, so I probably confided much more that I had intended. "Hunting is not for me; I don't know why I thought I'd be able to pull it off." The story had taken some time in telling. I stood up. "I guess I had better get home, Susan," I said and, offering her a hand, pulled her to an upright position. Carrying through on the momentum, she leaned into me and kissed me on the cheek.

"That was for good luck. I hope you'll be free to go to the dance Friday."

"I do too," I responded and realized that I meant it. There's no denying that Susan and I had been as close as siblings since childhood; she was the sister I never had. But on that afternoon, we walked back across the highway to West River Road unconsciously comfortable to be holding hands. When we reached 117 Nutmeg Lane, she dropped my hand and looked at me in a funny way. I hesitated. Normally I would have said, "So long," and turned toward the old homestead without a second thought, allowing her to get to the farm on her own.

"I'm really not in that big a hurry, would you mind if I walked you home?" I asked, and then turned the color of red raspberries.

At home, I went straight to my room and didn't come downstairs until dinner time. "Where's Dad?" I asked, noting his absence at the table.

"He was very upset. He looked everywhere for you; when he couldn't find you he took off. He said he had an urgent errand to run and would be late," mom said. "Sorry it didn't work out this morning."

"It's okay, I'll live," I responded grimly.

"You would have saved yourself a lot of grief if you had killed the rabbit, Bill," Michael said.

"I don't think so Mike. If I had killed that one, I would have been expected to go on killing them."

Chapter XXI

MISHAP AT DUGGAN'S

After the window-shattering incident, I had made up my mind that if I couldn't play ball at Duggan's Diamond, I wouldn't be a spectator there either. However, I left the dinner table in a fire-eating mood and feeling extravagantly rash. Breaking one of my own cardinal rules I went to the ball park to watch the Warriors and our archrivals, the Silver Arrows, play for the championship in the last game of the season. I would have given an eye-tooth to be in it.

By the time I got there it was dusk. The flood lights were on. The game was in the sixth inning and the score was five to three in favor of the Silver Arrows. In the seventh inning Lenny Schneider, our first baseman, sprained his ankle while at bat, putting the Warriors at a serious disadvantage. Larry gave me a look that I understood to be a plea for help. I struggled with my conscience, unable to make a firm decision one way or the other. Pete Fulton made up my mind for me. He came up to me with an ugly smirk on his face. "Too bad Daddy won't let his little boy play ball at Duggan's anymore," he taunted.

I shot him a killing look and turned to Larry. "Count me in," I said. "Lend me your mitt Lenny."

It was not the first time I had acted on impulse, but I couldn't recall ever being quite so flagrantly disobedient to my parents.

We gained a run in the eighth inning. Going into the bottom of the ninth inning the score stood at five to four in favor of our opponents. We had a man on first with two men out when I came up to bat. Pete Fulton was in the pitcher's box. It was a situation made in heaven – or hell, depending on the outcome. And I was it; the guy with three chances to make sandlot history in Redbud and beat the Silver Arrows to boot.

A gust of wind waltzed a dust eddy across the playing field. Laughing at an aside from the stands, I caught a mouthful of grit. I spat and wiped my mouth with the back of my hand. Then

I flexed my muscles, got nice and loose and stepped into the batter's box. Wriggling my backside, I crouched with the bat extended, poised and ready, waiting for Pete to go through his pitching ritual. He stalled in an attempt to rattle me. Hanging in there, I tuned him out and concentrated on what I had to do. Acting on a strong hunch that he was going to fire his fast ball on the first pitch, I braced for the zinger. Hauling back, gut muscles taut, mind razor sharp, I swung with all the strength and fury I had in me the instant the ball left his glove.

I heard the bat crack as it met leather and I knew the ball game was ours. I watched the ball sail past the glare of the lights and get lost in the night. An umpire put a bullhorn to his mouth and announced, "The ball game is over. The Warriors win six to five." The crowd roared and I received a standing ovation. I began to lope leisurely around the bases. The sense of elation must have lasted five seconds - maybe six - then above the din I heard the unmistakable sound of glass shattering and my ego dove from sky high to rock bottom in an instant.

Meanwhile, Bessie, one of the Campbell's prize cows had been running a fever for several days. The veterinarian assured Jim that it was just a mild case of cow pox and injected the animal with a new antibiotic that was supposed to clear up the infection in no time. Since cow pox is contagious, he instructed Jim to isolate Bessie from the rest of the herd and keep her in the barn for a couple of days. He provided the farmer with two repeat doses of the medication and departed.

Early on the day of the ball game, Bessie appeared slightly disoriented and ran a fever. As he had been instructed, Jim injected Bessie with a second dose of the medication. By eight o'clock that night, the cow's condition appeared critical; her temperature had shot up another couple of degrees, she lowed incessantly, and seemed extremely agitated.

Concerned, Jim led Bessie out of her small stall to the front end of the barn where the lighting was better and he was able to examine her more closely. The inside of her mouth was inflamed; other than that he could find nothing wrong. Once more he affixed a needle to a syringe and proceeded to inject the cow with the medication. The needle was still in her when it occurred to him that Bessie's erratic behavior might be caused by a reaction to the medicine.

Quickly, he removed the needle and reached for the phone on a nearby shelf to call the vet. As he did so, Bessie keeled over. Before Jim could get out of the way, he was knocked backward and inadvertently put his arm through a window, cutting it severely.

Peggy heard the glass break from inside the house. Without a moment's hesitation, she dashed out of the house and ran down the back steps. Then, noticing a baseball in her path, she stopped to pick it up put it in her apron pocket on her way to the barn. On a separate level of thinking, she believed the ball would serve as another piece of evidence in their case against Clarence Duggan.

The first thing she saw was the prone cow; then she saw her husband with a massive amount of blood on his arm. Quickly she dropped the ball to the ground and used her apron as a tourniquet.

"Get me to the emergency room in Plighton, Peg; we'll call the vet from there," Jim told her.

Usually mild mannered, Peggy wheeled the Dodge pickup out of the garage and, burning rubber, sped to the end of the driveway where she came to a screeching halt. Vehicles were parked haphazardly on both sides of the gate and along the road, forcing her to thread her way through them slowly and causing her to lose precious time. Frustrated, she lay on the horn and cursed the owners of them all. But who was to hear? The Warriors were carrying me around the diamond on their shoulders and the crowd was screaming wildly.

From my point of view, the victory was a hollow one. As soon as I could, I left the park and went to the farm. The road was long and lonely indeed. Warily I checked the greenhouse and saw no new breaks. There were lights on in the house, but when I knocked on the door, no one answered. I recalled then that Jed and Nora had planned to take the twins to a movie in Fenton that evening. Mincing forward on leaden feet, I headed for the barn. Entering through a side door, I found Bessie lying on the floor among evidence of a misdeed I mistakenly thought I had committed. The pieces fit the crime with remarkable certitude; the broken window, the spattering of blood in the area, the ball resting near Bessie's head, and the cow dead.

I was bewildered. How could I have hit a ball as far as the barn? It didn't make sense. Unless….? The only explanation I could think of was that the anger I had nursed from the hunt had been magnified by Pete Fulton's slur so much so that it had given me a moment of superhuman strength. Because of me the Campbell's prize cow was dead. In an exhibition of unbelievable anger I had killed Bessie.

Horrified, I picked up the ball and fled. Except to wash the blood off the ball in the river, I didn't stop running until I reached home. I could see through the window that the lights and the television were on in the living room so I knew someone was still up. Slipping into the house through the back door, I stood with a foot on the stairs and a hand on the railing. "Mom, Dad, I'm home," I called out as though all was right with the world.

"Get upstairs to bed, we'll talk in the morning," Dad called back in a surprisingly neutral tone of voice; a tone I didn't know how to interpret.

Chapter XXII

KEBOR'S MESA CALLS

Lying in bed, staring at the ceiling with my hands behind my head, I felt disenfranchised and so distressed that I didn't know if I wanted to go on living. As tense as a rivet and unable to sleep, I was conscious of every tick of the grandfather clock under the stairwell downstairs. I heard it chime the hour of nine - then ten - and then eleven.

Craving relief, I felt the tug of the mesa. For awhile I resisted its magnetic pull. There was no need to add to my liabilities by leaving the house in the middle of the night; especially since I had a ten o'clock curfew.

Like the chocolate you swear you will not eat, the harder I tried to deny the compulsion, the stronger the urge became to give in to it. Where else might I find solace?

When I could no longer stand the pressure, I threw the bed covers aside, dressed, and put a few essential in my knapsack. Heart beating madly, I tiptoed down the rear staircase, carefully skipping over the fifth step to avoid making it creak. Like a sneak thief, I stole out of the house into the cold autumn night and headed for Kebor's Mesa.

At another time I might have been afraid to enter the forest after dark; that night I was propelled by a fear greater than any the forest could produce. I paid no heed to the sounds of forest denizens as they scampered unseen. The watchful eyes of nocturnal predators held no terror for me. The piercing cry of the screech owl did not make me tremble, nor did the wind howling in the bowers above.

My eyes adjusted quickly to the darkness and I could see quite well as I traced the dimly lit trails, using the flashlight to guide me only through the most dense section of the forest and in places where shadows were deceptive. Upon reaching the crest of the ridge I paused to considerer the incline leading to the summit of the mesa before tackling it. The climb was tricky enough in the flush of day; the dark of the night could only multiply the difficulty. In my agitated frame of mind, I welcomed the challenge.

Since I needed both hands to negotiate the ascent, I put the flashlight back in the knapsack and, trusting my instincts and past experience, started up the trail, making sure my footing was on solid ground before shifting my weight. On the summit, I traced the winding trail to the pyramidal formation, and then branched off onto the path leading to the rock ledge where I willingly gave myself to its stony embrace.

There I sat in my favorite spot, eight hundred feet or so above the valley floor, gazing out at the Great Smokey Mountains. With my hands locked around my knees and my knees pulled up to my chin, I tried to make sense of the day's events. At fourteen years of age, I was bankrupt; a hopeless speck of humanity perched on the brink of the world, searching in vain for a way out of my troubles.

A myriad of stars shone brightly in a cloudless sky. Cascading waters, the string of lakes, and the Little Limerick River below, reflected silver in the light of a pale moon. Ebony silhouettes defined the rounded peaks of Mount Angel Head, Les Capitan's Fortress and Mount Rhoda. Save for the din of night creatures and the language of the wind in the trees, all was still.

As always, I sensed the power of the vast expanse. It held me in its spell and made me feel infinitesimally small and trivial. At the same time, it calmed me and helped me think more clearly.

Time and time again, my thoughts went through the day's events; from the morning's hunt to the mishap on the Campbell farm. The sight of Bessie lying dead in the barn was never out of mind. Something was oddly out of focus with the picture I projected, but for the life of me, I couldn't put a finger on it.

I pondered my predicament until my head throbbed and I could no longer think coherently. The chill in the air began to penetrate my clothing. Sternly, I told myself that I should return home before my absence was discovered. Still I lingered; my mind on my problems; my eyes on the stars glittering overhead, appearing like thousands of diamonds in a blue-black vault.

Suddenly, one of the points of light broke away from its fixed position in the sky and began to behave erratically. Bewildered, I unfolded my legs, leaned forward, and squinted. I thought it was a star and cupped a hand to my forehead to study the phenomenon more intently. No, it was not a star, I reasoned; stars do not do loops. Then what could it be? Was it a dare devil pilot testing a highly maneuverable military plane under the cover of night? Or, perhaps a mad scientist was also sitting under these same stars testing his latest toy by remote control.

Finally, I realized that the craft, whatever it might be, was in serious trouble. Fascinated, I watched it shorten the distance between us. As it drew closer it abruptly stopped, swerved, and shot upward. Just when I thought it was going to disappear from sight, it began to spiral downward again. At that point, the unbelievable happened; an entity, speaking in an alien language, contacted me telepathically.

"Please help me," was the message it conveyed.

It was strange to *hear* a string of weird syllables without the benefit of sound; and even stranger to have them translated automatically into a recognizable thought, as if by magic. And, as if by magic, I knew at once that the entity was of female gender

I had tickled the underbelly of mental telepathy on several occasions, but my capabilities were limited. For me, it either happened or it didn't; it wasn't something I could control or call up at will. Even so, every fiber of my being prompted me to respond to the plea for help, however odd it might be.

Doing as Dad had instructed me, I closed my eyes and concentrated hard on the alien being I now envisioned, trying to transmit my own thoughts into the ether.

"I'm Billy Briarwood. Are you real, or am I stuck in a dream? Besides, how could I possibly help you? You're up there, I'm down here, and levitation is not one of my strong suits."

"I will show you the way," the alien responded.

Ceasing to spiral, the object now hurtled straight toward earth at a tremendously fast rate of speed. I held my breath as suddenly, in seemingly no lapse of time, it made a ninety-degree turn, slid sideways across the horizon, and stopped to hover over Mount Angel Head. It continued to hover for a fraction of a second before plunging into the trees and tumbling end over end down the mountain side. In a blinding flash of light the show was over; the object had crashed somewhere on the far side of the river, almost in a direct line with my position on Kebor's Mesa. I watched for any signs of fire that may have resulted from the accident; but none ever materialized.

Minutes of eerie silence passed as I waited for further contact; then....

"Help me.... please."

"I would like to help you, but I don't know how. You see, I'm in trouble up to my armpits right now. I should be home in bed."

"Where is home?"

"I live in the Hollister House in the valley on the other side of this mesa," I said, pointing.

"Hmm, Billy Briarwood lives in the Hollister House. Interesting." Although the alien's musings were not meant for me to *hear*, somehow I picked up on them. "And *house* is *home*? Two words for one thing?"

"Well, yes, I guess so," I answered.

"You can help me, Billy; you have what I need in your pants pouch."

"Do you mean my pocket?"

"Yes, in your pocket. Help me and I promise to try to find a way to help you," the voice pleaded.

"Humph!" I snorted. "I'll help you if I can, but I doubt if you can help me; you don't know my father."

"What is your father's name," the entity asked.

"Paul…. Paul Briarwood," I answered.

"Come to me and I will look into this…. this Paul Briarwood."

"I saw the crash, but depth perception can be deceiving, especially at night. It might take a long time to find you."

"Time is irrelevant. However, if I am able I will beam a light from your flat-topped hillock to my ship; it will keep you on the right path."

I'd never had the mesa reduced to a hillock before, but…. okay, if that's the way she wanted it. Even as that thought was being formed, a much more potent one bombarded my mental processing system. She said *from* your flat-topped hillock *to* her ship, and not the other way around; in other words….

Leaping up, I brushed dried leaves from my clothing and swiftly scrambled from the ledge to the top of the summit to look in the direction of the big red sedimentary rock; the one embedded with shards of white stones. As though an electrical cord had been plugged into a circuit, a block of intense light suddenly materialized on the surface of the rock. The light began to stretch out and as it lengthened, it dimmed accordingly, ending on a spot low on the flank of Mount Angel Head. I had but to follow it.

Chapter XXIII

ELYCE

The telepathic voice, thunderous in its silence, was high-pitched and tremulous, yet silky; not unlike the musical tones resulting from a bow being drawn across the strings of a violin. The entity not only had the capacity to transmit thoughts; it was able to translate those thoughts into my language. Also, it had cleared up some of the mystery involving the shards of white stone. Could it explain the mesa as well?

I slipped the knapsack on my back and descended the north face of the mesa. At the base, I paused just long enough to get a reading on the beam of light with my compass just in case I lost sight of it on the way. Fording the icy cold water of the Little Limerick River without getting my clothing wet required removing my shoes and socks and rolling up my pant legs above the knees. It had been a number of years since I had gone barefoot in the summer, so my feet were tender and didn't welcome the feel of the stony river bottom. On the opposite bank I dried my feet with an old diaper, such as mom used as cleaning cloths, and replaced my footwear.

I discovered quickly that following the beam of light did not mean traveling in a straight line. Often, the beam was interrupted by a rock formation or some other dense object, making it necessary for me to circumvent the obstacle and search for the beam again on the opposite side. As long as the beam was above me, angling down from the top of the mesa, it was easy to find in the night sky; however, as I traveled onward, the beam came closer to ground level, making the task of keeping it in sight increasingly difficult. Somehow I managed.

Sometimes whistling just to hear the sound and sometimes with mouth agape, I proceeded past unique outcroppings, overhanging cliffs, and spring-fed rills that trickled down stone terraces. Mysterious looking caverns with fiercely black interiors did not arouse my need to know. At times passage became extremely rugged, forcing me to find my way around sheer stone walls and ascend and descend steep grades.

As the night progressed, it struck me that I had gone a long distance since leaving the mesa.

Suddenly, everything seemed surreal. I felt disoriented and deeply troubled. Home never seemed so far away. When I reached an area with a clear view of my surroundings, I turned and trained my vision toward the south. From this perspective, I easily found the distinctive flat top of Kebor's Mesa, standing out like the oddity it was in the glow of the moon. The sight gladdened my heart and prompted me to concentrate harder on gaining my destination and, thus, finalizing my mission.

Perhaps several hundred feet or so ahead of me I came upon broken boughs and bruised shrubbery and knew that I was nearing the site of the crash. Yards ahead the beam of light ended.

I was already over-stressed; now, to have reached my goal brought forth a sudden gale of insane laughter, and when the laughter subsided, I folded like an accordion. Curled up on the ground, I blubbered uncontrollably. Tears, the safety valve for human emotions, brought considerable relief and, for a moment, I let them flow freely.

Once I had regained my equilibrium I approached the mass of forest debris furtively and, with a hand cupped around an ear, I listened guardedly. Then, padding quietly, I drew closer; and closer still. Cautiously I made a move to part the foliage, and then quickly stepped back. The possibility that I would not come away alive was an ever present threat. Breathing deeply I finally dredged up sufficient courage to part the torn branches and peer between them. There, as God is my witness, stood a pink flying machine, resting on three legs with not a bolt out of place. Naturally, I was dumbfounded.

The alien communicated mentally from inside the craft. " You are Billy?"

"Yes," I replied, holding my distance.

"You are young, Billy, doing a man's job."

"I'm fourteen."

"Fourteen what?" the alien asked in its own way.

Thinking quickly, I answered, "Fourteen revolutions around the sun."

This was followed by what I thought sounded like alien laughter; a violin producing titillating notes, if you can imagine that. "I believe

The Riddle of Kebor's Mesa

that would be years," she said, making me feel like an idiot.

The craft, no more than twelve feet in diameter, was covered with a pink metallic fabric. It stood on three retractable legs with large feet that toed out; for stability when landing, I learned later. A wide ring encircled the midsection of the machine. It displayed portholes framed in a bronze-like metal, the centers of which appeared to be solid disks. The portholes were spaced just inches apart. The domed turret on top of the machine was composed of a clear thick pink substance resembling Plexiglas. It was polished to a mirror finish, giving me the notion that it had one-way visibility.

There wasn't a scratch on the machine to indicate that it had crash landed. The charred earth I expected to find at the site was sorely lacking. Judging by the sensation coursing through my body, the alien craft was pulsing with energy, but gave no tangible evidence to verify it.

"Nice ship," I said.

At my comment, the ring on the craft began to rotate. When it stopped, a disk slid aside in one of the portholes to reveal a camera. The camera focused on me.

"Oh, what a lovely primitive species," I understood the alien to say.

In a phrase, she downgraded me to a cave-dweller with a brain the size of a pea. Primitive, indeed! Raising my chin defiantly, I reminded the alien – in thought - why I was there. "I've come to help you, but if you don't think I'm capable...."

"I detect hostility. I did not mean to offend you. I am desperate for your help," it returned on the same wave length. "Would you like to come aboard, Billy?"

"No, you and your machine frighten me," I answered at once. Standing in front of a UFO, conversing telepathically with an alien is not your ordinary Sunday afternoon game of croquet. I felt wary and totally outside my scope of reasoning. My mind raced. My heart beat faster than normal. I expected to see a half dozen little green men pop out of the bushes any second and take me aboard the ship whether I wanted to go or not.

"Then let us resolve this quickly and I'll be on my way," she said, "I need what you have in your pants pouch…., pocket; or, perhaps I should say in the little box in your pocket."

Obliging her, I opened the cricket box Grandpa Hollister made for me and emptied its contents onto the palm of my hand - seven silver dimes and three crystal beads. This time she did not convey words, but the excitement she transmitted sent me reeling.

Again, the ring girding the machine rotated, bringing to the fore another porthole that opened up to display a matter I cannot adequately describe. It appeared to be made up of countless iridescent particles all of which were in a frenzy of motion.

"Insert the pieces of white ore and crystal orbs into the port," I was told.

"How can I comply when the port has a solid barrier?" I asked.

"The port may look solid, Billy, but what you see is a force field. Whenever a disk is shunted aside, the port automatically activates the force field to keep my ship hermetically sealed. The

The Riddle of Kebor's Mesa

force field prevents the atmosphere inside from becoming contaminated with foreign substances. It also purifies anything passing through it. Be assured it will receive your objects at a touch."

Her voice had lost the squeal in it that a violin can produce. Now I heard only the dulcet, melodic strains of the instrument. It had a soothing effect on me. My fears dissipated. I was faced with the fact that the creature was about to take my beads and coins and fly away, leaving me with a thousand unanswered questions. I hesitated.

"There are things about you that puzzle me," I began, quite timidly to be sure.

"You are curious about the mint condition of the ship and the blinding light you saw. Is that correct?" she interjected mutely.

"That's true. I expected to find a wreck and evidence of a fire," I replied. "And too, I would like to know about the beam of light. How did it connect to the shards of white stone? And about the mesa; do you know why it is flat?"

"If I explain, will you insert the orbs and the ore?"

"I guess so," I said, unhappy about the myriad of questions that would go unexplored.

"Since our technology outshines yours it would be absurd to expect you to understand our scientific language. I'm not sure you will understand everything in layman terms, but I'll do my best. You see, our technology allows us to travel at warp speed and come to a full stop, or reverse direction, without slowing down; it is that advanced. Likewise, our ships have been incorporated with an extensive network of safety features. The very instant the ship went out of control, I issued a command to which the ship, of course, responded immediately. The split second before impact, a discharge of negative energy stopped the forward motion of the ship and prevented it from crashing. The earth's atmospheric conditions, together with the discharge, produced luminescent sparking; that is the burst of light you saw. Luminescent sparking is similar to heat lightening, except that it is a form of cold light," she told me.

"Hmm, how do I explain the shards of white stone? Well, first of all you must understand that we are not speaking of shards of white stone, but of an ancient design for a cosmic booster. Picture an electrical cord that is attached to an appliance; the appliance doesn't function until it is plugged into an electrical outlet. In my case the appliance is the space ship, the electrical cord is an invisible current extending from the ship, and the electrical outlet is the cosmic booster."

"Did your species flatten the mesa?"

"We did; thousands of years ago. Long before a civilization existed here, we lopped off one-third of the hillock, scattered it around, and planted our cosmic boosters. Each one of them contained enough cosmic energy to kick-start a space ship into the upper stratosphere. We have a more modern system now so I am fortunate that the last one here had enough power left to guide you to me. You see, the booster is designed to retain its power over several millennia; however, the older it gets the more quickly its power drains once it is tapped into.

"Gosh!" I managed, overawed by her information. Although starved for additional dialogue, I remained true to my word; without further delay I held the beads and coins up to the port and watched as they were *absorbed*.

Apparently, she was efficient and knew what she was doing; in an instant two crystal beads and five silver dimes were shunted back to me.

"I used only what I needed – one crystal orb and two pieces of white ore. Thank you, Billy Briarwood, I did not take advantage of your generosity." Again, I heard the impression of musical laughter. "How easily I pick up on your thoughts. The orbs to you are crystal beads, and the pieces of white ore are silver coins. I'll try to remember. Would you consider trading a bead and three coins for a Polduntarian medal? It would be reassuring to have the material aboard the ship in case I need it."

Polduntarian? Was she referring to an alloy, a place, a being? What? "Oh, yeah, I'd really like that," I said, warming up to the strange entity. Despite our differences, I now considered the entity a friend and possessed a strong desire to make closer contact with it. Besides making a great souvenir and giving credence to the tale I'd have to tell when I got home again – if I got home again - the medal would have real sentimental value as a reminder of this exceedingly rare experience. As requested, I put a bead and three coins into the port and in return received a most unusual medal.

The medal was made of the same material used on the shell of the craft. One side of the medal displayed an embossed star cluster, and the reverse depicted, also in bas relief, what appeared to be an eight-spoke wagon wheel.

"The medal is beautiful," I said earnestly. "What is represented by the star cluster and the wagon wheel?" Later, much later, I would recall the mental exchange and marvel that it had come to me so clearly and so easily. Could it have been the alien's influence? I choose to think so.

"It is not a wagon wheel, but a symbol we use to illustrate the many areas of the universe," she informed me. The star cluster represents the galaxy your astronomers call Triangulum. The largest star in the cluster symbolizes my home planet, Polduntar. I must go there now."

"Wait!" I cried in protest. "I don't know your name, or what you look like, or anything, and…. and you said you'd help me."

"Unless you come aboard, I cannot get you home before you leave, Billy; however, I will do what I can from afar."

"Can't you come out so I can see you?" I asked, sighing with disappointment.

"I could, but it wouldn't be wise. The machine and I are perfectly attuned. I already had one mishap because of my negligence; I don't want to risk another.

"There is no way then…. I was hoping…."

"You are still welcome to come aboard; no harm would befall you. You saved my life and my ship…." The creature paused momentarily, and then as further inducement said, "When will you ever get another chance?"

That last remark sold me. "I guess I do want to meet you face to face and see the inside of your ship."

"I had hoped from the start that our meeting would not be aborted quickly. I am as curious about you as you are about me. Permit me to prepare you. First I must scan your brain to learn all about you, then when you come aboard you get to ask all of the questions; deal?"

The ring on the machine rotated and I was confronted with yet another porthole. In this instance when the disk slid back it revealed an apparatus that looked like the shower head in my bathroom at home. The thing snaked toward me on the end of a flexible cord and settled close to the top of my head. As though floating on a bubble of air, it moved slowly over my entire skull area, making faint clicking sounds at split second intervals. Meekly, I submitted to the in-depth probe, too numb to know fear.

"You may now come aboard my ship, William Briarwood."

The door was indiscernible and could not be opened until a section of the ring folded back on a hinge, and then the door opened from the top, forming a ramp. A curtain, alive with the same iridescent particles I'd observed in one of the ports, caused me to balk.

Noticing my reaction, the creature prodded me further. "It is essential that you enter through the force field, Billy. Do not be afraid," she said.

From habit, I brushed my clothing, tucked my shirt in, and ran fingers through my hair, and then, as though hypnotized, I entered.

All communication with the alien to this point had been conducted telepathically; even the impressions of her voice were manifestations in my mind rather than actual sounds. Now we spoke in conventional audible voices; hers chiming sweetly, and mine that of a boy most of the time, but now and then, without warning, changing to the husky voice of an adult male.

Save for the cranium and eyes, the creature before me was incredibly pale and translucent; ethereal and pretty in an alien way. She stood about four feet tall, was slight of build and had, of course, unique features. The cap-like affair covering the cranium was golden brown and had the appearance of paper-thin tortoise shell. It hugged the base of her neck at the back, but protruded above the eyes in the fashion of a bulky visor. The translucency and color of her extremely large eyes reminded me of amber. They dominated an expressionless face. I saw nothing that resembled a nose. A round mouth that opened and closed like the shutter on a camera was centrally located in the area below the eyes. Appendages, extending from either side of her head where you would expect to find ears, had feathery endings that were constantly in motion. Her legs were long compared to her short slim torso. Both legs and arms were without joints, but flexed freely at her whim. A swan-like neck tapered to shoulders that had little definition. A garment as sheer as gossamer clothed this lovely creature whose movements were graceful and fluid, giving me to believe she was almost weightless and without any distinctive bone material in her body.

A cube, the size of a mustard seed, was attached to the temporal region of the head immediately below the left appendage. I took it for granted that this cube was the means by which she spoke my tongue. Last, but certainly not least, she was bathed in a white glow that made me want to genuflect with reverence.

Again, I dared to be bold. "Do you have a sense of smell?" I asked.

"Yes, of course," she said, and tilted her head back to show me the four slits above the eyes in the base of the cranium cover.

In a rapid glance around I saw no furnishings or creature comforts.

"There is no requirement," she said, reading my mind.

The inner walls of the craft were lined with an opalescent material. Peculiar symbols, made up of precious jewels and metals, decorated the inside of the dome. Below the dome, an extravaganza of highly sophisticated instrumentation was built into the entire circumference of the machine's interior. Much of it consisted of panels of small blinking lights and intricate contrivances set in motion; spinning spheres suspended in stilted glass bowls, small metal bellows opening and closing at precise intervals, and pivoting arms that moved rings smoothly up and down the length of shiny metal rods. One section of wall was devoted to disks that rotated clockwise and counterclockwise in rhythmic sequence.

The largest piece of technological gadgetry held me enthralled and, of course, I was curious. I wanted to know everything there was to know about the alien and the flying machine at once, but that was not to be.

"I'm Elyce. As you can see, unlike yourself, I am highly evolved. Your spirit is laden with much matter. And yes, I am the female of my species, but not in the text that you know. My species does not reproduce the way your species does. And we do not harbor sentimental feelings such as you possess for Susan."

Recalling Susan's parting kiss, my hand went to my cheek at once. "You.... you know about Susan?"

"You opened your mind to me, Billy; of course I know about Susan. I also know that your problems are not as they seem. But first, let me explain, by walking through the force field you were hygienically and atmospherically adapted to the interior of this ship. You can survive in here comfortably for the duration of your stay. Oh, don't be alarmed," she said, quick to assess my thoughts, "your stay will be limited and, as I promised, I will get you home before you leave."

This was the second time she mentioned getting me home before I left. "I don't understand," I said.

"Eons ago my people unraveled the mystery of time and space, or rather time/space, the continuum. Penetrating other-world dimensions is an integral part of our existence. Since you are a seeker of truth, I'd like to take you to a place I know that exists at the hub of the universe. To get there we will need to cut through several dimensions and cover more space than if we adhered to the well traveled route. In effect, we'll be traveling faster than the speed of light. So, for a fraction of our journey, we'll reverse the hands of time. By making the correct calculations, I'll get you home before you left," she said yet again.

And again, I said, "I don't understand."

"Think of it as a bicycle ride to school. You can get from home to school in Britt's Bay across country almost as quickly as the bus that weaves in and out of neighborhoods to get there."

"That's true," I said, trying to measure up to her depth of understanding.

Abruptly, Elyce threw her hands up much the way a human would, except her hands – and her arms as well – had the grace and flexibility of a sea anemone. "Ah, my manners are lacking; I forgot you must be nourished. Afterward, we'll relax and I'll try to answer your many questions about me and the ship. Afterward, I'll take you on a ride you'll never forget, okay?" she said, and with a gesture, suggested that I might sit on the floor of the ship if I wished.

"Okay," I said and remained standing, dubious about the food she was about to serve since I didn't see anything edible. As it turned out, I neither received the five-course meal I was accustomed to having at home, nor did I get to linger over dessert.

For a fraction of a second, no more, Elyce posed with serene elegance in front of a piece of equipment that might have been a headlight taken from the family car, except that it was riddled with tiny holes. At a slight nod from her, the object showered me with tiny threads of light. At once, I felt completely rejuvenated; energetically fit and calorie satisfied.

It would have made a fine Christmas present for Mom, I thought, except we didn't have an outlet for the thing.

The Riddle of Kebor's Mesa

"I'm curious. What is that contraption?" I asked, motioning toward the bulky bank of assorted hardware.

"That is called an intellecapacitor. Actually, it is a multi-functional piece of highly technical equipment that coordinates nine distinct computerized operations within the ship, distinguished by the nine separate windows you see, stacked three on three.

"The center window controls the camera, which incidentally has the capacity to perform a multitude of tasks. It can look through objects as well at them; detect pollutants; register temperatures, atmosphere, and wind velocities. It can also calculate great distances based on star readings. Each of the eight windows surrounding the center one performs in conjunction with the camera as well as having a number of other diverse functions aside from it," she explained. "Although separated by partitions the functions are interconnected by very fine tubes filled with Mercury."

One of the windows illustrated several mini-size plungers that moved up and down through a clear substance with the viscosity of heavy oil.

Another exhibited the constant expansion and contraction of a large bubble encased in a blue vacuum. Still a third contained dozens of minuscule lights, linked by wire to each other and the Mercury tubes she mentioned. These too, blinked incessantly. So smoothly did it all run, there wasn't a sound to be heard other than an occasional faint click.

"How are you able to repair the damages when you…. when you have such delicate hands?" I asked, putting a hand out and curling my fingers into a fist to illustrate the grasping ability it had. By comparison, her hands had three short tapered fingers that appeared incapable of performing any delicate operation.

"This intellecapitator is light years ahead of the computers you use on earth, Billy. All of the equipment you see here is programmed to respond to my mental and verbal commands. The right command will get any job done," Elyce informed me.

"I don't see any storage space. Where do you keep your fuel and what kind do you use?"

"This ship does not burn fuel," she said and went on to give me a discourse on some of the dynamics employed by the engineers and scientists on Polduntar.

I was like an oak seedling trying to have an intelligent discussion with a redwood giant. I did not comprehend her rhetoric or many of the technical terms she used to define the mechanics of the ship and its parts, but I have recorded what I can recall. Let it be known; however, I make no claim to absolute accuracy.

She talked about pressure-exerting components that had the capacity to convert and reconvert molecular structure. She expounded on negative energy, ionizers, gyroscopiclegislators, and interstellar communication systems. She covered the functions of a number of stabilizing "doohickeys" and rotating "thingamajigs." Other topics included star thrust, grid shifts, dimensional gravity, the push and pull of universal tides, and the use of solar and intergalactic wind tunnels. She explained about "fixing" on a point in time/space, "locking in," and getting there *NOW*.

"Centrifugal force and momentum are invaluable tools. When we take off, the ship will spin away from the earth, describing ever greater loops. Somewhere within that spiraling configuration lies the secret of "cutting corners" in space. The distance from here to there in time/space is not a straight line, but a decidedly curved one.

Dazzled by her display of superior knowledge, I shook my head; she was rapidly making my brain weary. "Your wisdom is beyond me. Perhaps a category other than the machine or time/space....?" I said. "How did the accident occur?"

"Since your planet has become so populated, we seldom land on it anymore; we observe it from outer space. I had the misfortune of getting caught in a meteor shower after inadvertently neglecting to place the protective disk cover on an open port. By chance a tiny meteor penetrated the force field, damaged the balance control on the intellecapacitor and sent me plummeting. Built in safety features immediately went into play and the ship landed safely, yes; but I still needed you, dear primitive friend, to bring me the necessary elements to repair the damage. You came to my rescue, and I'm grateful.

For a fleeting moment I allowed myself to consider Elyce objectively; wondering how my human counterparts would treat her if she should happen to fall into their hands. Would they treat this delicate creature with hostility? Would they wish to harm her? Would they even recognize her advanced level of existence?

Chapter XXIV

ELYCE'S PHILOSOPHY

"Was my mission preordained? Was it meant to be?" I asked. "The crystal beads and silver coins were in my possession for a long time. I have always considered them special."

At the moment, Elyce was pacing around on one foot, as it were. "I don't know," she said, "it's a possibility since you are a seeker of truth. Still, some things must remain a mystery; even to me as enlightened as I am."

"What have you learned about us humans?"

"The surface of your planet is undergoing drastic change, Billy. Technology is advancing rapidly. Some of the revelations are beneficial to your species, others are not. When I return to my home planet my findings will be studied by scholars much wiser and more elevated than I.

They will render judgment. I am not qualified to do that. Your planet does seem to be in serious trouble; surely you know that."

"Yes, the pollution," I volunteered.

"It is not just the pollution; many of your species have lost sight of the overall good. They are out of touch with the stream of higher consciousness. They are not learning the lessons they were put on earth to learn; that is, love and respect for each other, and care for the blue sphere on which you dwell."

"Suppose we don't change for the better?"

"Universally speaking, it doesn't matter. Nothing really matters in terms of creation. The Supreme Power, or God-force as you call it, *IS* the universe and we are all a part of it. It is so perfect, it adjusts to the tiniest incident; compensates for the smallest act. The enlightenment an individual gains in a lifetime is their responsibility. We have forever, you know, but never fear, there is no escape; we can only reap what we have sown."

"That is an old bromide that I've heard often. Did you pick it out of my brain?" I asked with a wry smile.

"Your species is amusing," she said, ignoring my remark. "They believe that if they aren't caught committing wrongful acts, they are free of retribution; how mistaken they are. Every deed, every thought is etched on your soul. The soul designates who you are. Everything you are, everything you stand for is what you take with you when you leave your world."

"Then we are judged after death," I stated with an air of conviction.

"You judge yourself," she said. "Death is not what you think. It is an awakening; a warm, loving, wonderful homecoming. Shepherding souls are ready to welcome you, console you, and help you over the stumbling blocks of leaving your earthbound vehicle."

"But, you said...."

"I said that we pay, and we do. When we leave our mortal vehicle for good, we see ourselves as we really are. Each man judges himself based on who he is and what he is."

"Who decides where we go when we die?"

"You do. Like attracts like, whether you are talking about molecules or human souls, it makes no difference. As an example, your fish and birds of a kind migrate toward each other. Sharks do not swim with minnows, nor do eagles fly with sparrows. Sinners migrate toward sinners and saints toward saints. Upon death murderers will cast themselves with murderers. Their punishment will be to see themselves in those who surround them.

"As I said, there is no escape. While on earth you create your own future in the hereafter. You are the author of your own destiny so to speak. It is not negotiable, or complicated, but it is the final word. And it is fair, don't you think?" She hesitated. "Don't be glum. All are redeemed. The vilest sinner will flail himself until he has wiped the slate clean and is free to try again."

"Do you know what you are saying to be the absolute truth, or is it your idea of the truth?" I asked.

"It is what I and all of like-thinking Polduntarians in my particular belief system perceive to be the truth; the belief on which we pattern our lives," she answered. "You see, Billy, we are all connected through the stream of higher consciousness. Only by immersing ourselves in the stream, as you have done, and earnestly seeking truth can we hope to grow in understanding. What is beyond the stream, I do not know. My existence is on a plane above yours, but even so, we are not so different. Other systems on my planet may contradict what I hold to be true, but we do not fight over the variances; instead, we try to reconcile our differences.

"We might be compared to microbes on the bottom of the sea, trying to determine what it is that disturbs the water on the surface. As highly evolved as we consider ourselves to be, we constantly seek greater insight into the mysteries that continue to elude us. We, too, want to know more about the Supremacy of which we are a part." She paused momentarily. "Well, I hope you understand what I have told you."

"How is it possible for me to be a part of…. well, say a star a million light years away?"

"Hmm, you have many intellectual boundaries, so I know this is difficult for you. You think of God, or the God-force, as being separate from the whole, but that is not so. The God-force

IS. The totality of the universe *IS.* You and I *ARE.* The stars *ARE.* She noticed the perplexed look on my face and sighed an alien sigh.

"Let me see if I can equate this to you in a way you will understand. Think of a food your mother makes that requires a number of ingredients."

"Bread pudding," I said at once, "with raisins and pecans."

"I see, stale bread; bread made from a refined grain product. I don't comprehend why your species removes the nutrients from the kernels of wheat and eats the white dust that remains. Anyway, your mother uses bread and egg – egg is high in protein which you need – salt, raisins, nuts, milk, and sugar. Have I named everything in your foodstuff, Billy?"

"Mom puts cinnamon and nutmeg in it, too," I told her.

"Cinnamon and nutmeg ground fine for flavor; yes, that would make it taste better. All these things put together make bread pudding; am I right, Billy?"

"Yes," I replied.

"Each ingredient in the pudding has but one responsibility; to be itself. A raisin must be a raisin. A nut must be a nut. The egg, even though it is mixed up with everything else, is still egg. And yet, the sum of the mixture is bread pudding.

"Aren't you over simplifying?" I asked.

"Only to make a point; you do understand what I'm illustrating, don't you?"

"Yes."

"There, see, I've made a point.

"You mentioned that the symbol of the eight-spoke wheel on the Polduntarian medal you gave me represents the many arms of the universe. I'm curious about that; what does it mean exactly?"

"Hmm, it means....," she began and hesitated for a short spell as she drifted around, feather-like, from spot to spot. "It means that there are places in the universe where galaxies and space materials in varying stages of development exist in astronomical quantities and extend to fathomless reaches. Our scientists refer to them as arms of the universe; some refer to them as islands of star activity. Surrounding these many universes are the space deserts; oceans of nothingness; black voids where Aytozee continually creates new worlds.

"Aytozee?" I questioned, thinking she was getting cute with me, "Ay to Zee?" I couldn't keep from laughing.

"What is so different between 'Aytozee' and 'Alpha and Omega'? Or, 'Creator' for that matter?" she came back at me, emitting a series of musical notes which indicated that she, too, had a sense of humor.

"Aytozee," I repeated, "seems to be synonymous with God-force; outside of the universal whole. Could that be?" I asked, glancing at her slyly.

"No, no, it is Aytozee's function to create; just as it is the function for yeast to cause bread to rise," she answered with a tinge of annoyance in her voice. "Aytozee is the most supreme of the supreme; but still a part of the whole."

In my predicament, levity was a luxury so I grew serious swiftly. "If you are aware that new worlds are being created, perhaps you can answer another question. I believe there are stars beyond the stars that I can see on a clear dark night; and more stars even farther away. Tell me, Elyce, does the universe go on forever? My imperfect intellect does not allow me to visualize that in which endlessness is a reality. It is my understanding that all things must come to an end. By the same token, I cannot imagine the opposite either. When I try to picture a universe that ceases to be somewhere on the edge of space, I am compelled to wonder what is on the far side of those limits. "See? I am mystified."

"I honestly don't know; that is something I ponder myself," she said, and lapsed into silence; a delicate hand reaching for a feathery earlobe. Then, "You have a brilliant mind, Billy, maybe there is hope for your kind."

Embarrassed, I quickly changed the subject. "Tell me, what is your planet like, Elyce?"

"Keep in mind, there are many realities. Polduntar is the farthest planet from the Hermaxus sun star system within the Triangulum Galaxy. Your scientists would proclaim it uninhabitable. Compared to earth, it is a young planet and the surface is tumultuous; fire on one side and ice on the other. We dwell mostly in the area between. Because we are composed mostly of spiritual non-matter, neither temperature extremes nor atmospheric conditions affect us. In our sexual encounters, we may literally become one with our chosen mate; a sublime sensation I've heard. If we wish, we may remain unified and go through a ritual that will produce an offspring before we will our molecules to separate and we become individuals again. We value our spirituality and superior knowledge highly and have successfully integrated both into our technology, enabling us to achieve miraculous feats. It took many millennia; but this is the end result," she related with a flourishing bow.

"Are you happy?"

"Indeed! I thoroughly enjoy my reality." She stopped and considered her last statement. "Yes, that's right, there's my reality, your reality, and many other realities, depending upon the order of the world you chance to be in. However, there is but one ultimate reality. From what I have learned from scouting the inhabited planets scattered about the heavens, we simply evolve according to the conditions we exist in. Thus, though we seek our God from various aspects of the universe, we are all searching for the same ultimate truth; that is all."

"When I get home again, I don't know if I'll be able to handle everything you've taught me. You've quieted a yearning deep inside me. I don't see you as an alien, but rather as a truly…., truly…."

"Say what is on your mind, Billy, you needn't feel ill at ease."

"I see you as a very lovely creature. I think I love you. Am I being silly?"

"Not at all, we may be light years apart in one way; but we are kindred spirits in another," she said. "I love you, too."

"Thanks," I said and looked longingly into her amber pools. Liquid and mesmerizing, they tempted me to dive into them and be lulled in the bosom of her advanced knowledge. With a jerk, I diverted my gaze and took a step toward safer ground. "I know it's impolite to ask a lady her age, but would you mind telling me how old you are?"

"I am not much older than you in terms of a lifetime, but you see, I recall other lifetimes and I know that when I shed this vehicle, I will be born again. And so, I remember being as young as a raindrop; however I am probably as old as the oldest star," she stated matter-of-factly, and then began to make a circuit of the ship. Immediately, the ship's control panels and the moving parts on the intellecapacitor displayed increased activity.

"It's time for our ride, Billy," she said, laughing her tinkling little laugh. "This little dimension-breaker will transport us into an altered reality before you can think 'pink.'"

There was a sudden burst of power, and in an instant, Elyce and I were on the far side of the earth's ionosphere. Another burst of power put us in the outer reaches of the Milky Way, hell bent for an incredible journey into deep space. Weightless, we floated in the dome of the ship and took in realms of celestial wonder.

Expertly, she brought the pink craft to a stop in the middle of nowhere. "This is the hub of the universe, or Sea of Eternity as we know it," she explained, "where thought, consciousness, and the spark of life itself, originate. It is safe to leave the ship here while we take a romp, Billy."

Bidding the door open, she floated down the ramp with me close behind. Before taking off I looked back at the flying machine and saw that my corporeal self had been left in the ship's chamber.

"Are you aware of the silver cord?" she asked.

I nodded, knowing she referred to the soul's attachment to the navel. It would not break away from the body until the moment of death.

"It is your passport back to the ship," she informed me, taking hold of my hand, "so feel free to stretch, Billy. Stretch and listen to the drone of solar winds. Ride them. Reach for a star and don't be afraid; I won't lose you."

I saw a liquid sky, bluer than the blue of the deep ocean, wherein all of the yesterdays and tomorrows fused with the here and now and came within my grasp. For one infinitesimal moment in time, I understood completely the eternal quality of our souls, and what it meant to be one with the universe.

Stretching, I spread myself as fine as mist and then stretched some more until I spanned a hundred light years. In that state, I swam through colorful curtains of dazzling light to reach for a star; and then I was that star, glowing brilliantly with power and energy. The experience was so joyfully ecstatic it pained me. Still, I wanted more; however, at that juncture, a supernal guardian approached from a place unknown and commanded me it to collect my spirit.

The next thing I knew, my spirit had again assumed its earthly form and I was drifting with Elyce toward her flying machine.

"We have a little time to spare," she said in an attempt to console me. "Listen carefully and you'll hear the cradle song of creation and the litany of the ancients chanting for the redemption of lost souls."

Her description was probably more refined than mine, but when I listened, I heard the euphonious sounds of echoes and reverberations caused by churning cosmic matter that engulfed time immemorial. The clash of cymbals and the roll of thunderous drums underscored the everlasting day as fireworks on an empyreal scale exhibited stars exploding into existence while others disappeared before my eyes.

Holding a hand oddly with little substance, I remained close to Elyce who observed as a matter of course.

"Will I be able to come here after I die?" I wanted to know.

"This is part of my reality, Billy. You have to evolve to my level of existence before you may luxuriate in a time/space adventure on your own. If there are greater things than this to behold, I am not aware of them. Your species, and some of mine, speak of spirituality, but have no real concept of the true meaning of this remarkable quality in all of us. Remember what you have witnessed when you're again in your own reality."

"I'm not ready to go back; there are things we haven't discussed yet."

"You have to go back, and the time is now."

She spoke the words and, mysteriously, we were back in the ship without having experienced any conscious effort to get there. My spirit also was restored to its corporeal self. I was a flesh-and-blood human again.

In a dizzying blur of motion, the pink flying machine eclipsed the distance from the Sea of Eternity to Mount Angel Head in seconds.

"I will always remember you, Billy. When you propose marriage to Susan, do so on the summit of the flat hillock; tell her of our adventure and I will confirm your story," she said, flashing a little round smile. "And think about the window in the barn. Sorry to rush you but we must say 'Goodbye.'"

"No, wait! I have another question….."

"There isn't time, Billy, go quickly," she said, "and now 'Goodbye, Billy.' Billiee…., Billieeee…."

Chapter XXV

BACK TO EARTH

"Billy! Billy! It's time to get up; breakfast in twenty minutes," dad called up the front stairwell; his voice urgent, but remarkably cheerful.

"Coming, Dad," I called back drowsily. Then with a start, I sat up in bed and swiftly scanned the room. Everything appeared to be as it had been when I went to bed the night before. I was wearing the same pajamas. The clothing I had worn the day before was still piled on a chair where I left them before going to bed. And my knapsack was hanging on a wall peg where I always kept it.

The last thing I remembered from the deep-space experience was hearing Elyce say "Goodbye." How did get I from her pink flying machine to my bed? I rubbed my eyes; could it all have been a dream? I tossed the covers back and ran to the pile of clothing to retrieve the cricket box from my pants pocket. Not even daring to breathe, I slid the cover back. The cricket box now contained one crystal bead, two silver dimes, and one pink Polduntarian medal.

Clasping the medal in the palm of my hand, I raised my eyes to the heavens and thanked the God-force that led me to Elyce. Briefly, I basked in the glory that had been mine, blew Elyce a kiss, and wondered where one reality leaves off and another one begins.

With my head in the clouds and doubting that my feet would ever again touch ground, I showered, donned my Sunday best and skipped lightly down the stairs, prepared to face whatever fate awaited me.

At the doorway to the kitchen, I paused. The family, including David and Arlene, were seated at the table, waiting for me. Among all the smiling faces, Dad's smile was the broadest. Weird.

"Come, take your place, there's something for you on your chair," he said, flashing one of those ice-melting lop-sided grins of his.

I walked around the table to my customary spot and, sure enough, there was a package on my chair; wrapped in birthday paper and tied with a blue ribbon.

"What is this?" I asked. "It's not my birthday."

"Open it," Dad said.

To say I had mixed feelings is putting it mildly. Evidently, Dad hadn't heard about Bessie, the Campbell's prize cow. With deliberate control, I removed the ribbon and paper and opened the box. I took the enclosed card out of the envelope and commenced to read.

"Read it out loud, Billy." Mom's request echoed around the table.

This is what I read: "Happy belated birthday to the son who insists on marching to the thump of his own heartbeat. Yesterday, after our so-called hunting trip, I had time to think. I put myself in your shoes and considered what I would have done in your situation; follow an order or be true to my principles. Living up to your principles clearly defines the man you are Billy. I had no right to try to force you to engage in a family tradition you detest. I am awfully proud of you. You have definitely earned the rite of passage into manhood; you merely entered through a different door. Love, Dad." A post script read: "All five shots hit the "O" in my sign; you owe me."

Right then, my feet hit the floor and I knew I was home.

"Show us what you got, Billy," Arlene said.

Stemming a flow of tears, I displayed a nifty camera equipped with a zoom lens and a flash attachment. Unable to contain them any longer, tears flowed unchecked as I went and hugged Dad with all my might. "It's the perfect gift for me. Thanks, Dad, I love it, but I love you more."

"I thought you might like a camera. Incidentally, Ricky Sullivan told his father everything that happened at the ball game last night and his father told me. It was too bad about Lenny's ankle, but I'm glad you didn't let Pete Fulton bully you. You did what any man would have done; however, you won't be tempted anymore. We're putting Clarence Duggan out of business. Without naming names, he was seen counting out five hundred dollars in bills and entering two hundred dollars in his ledger. An IRS audit will take care of him," he said. "Jim and I have plans for a baseball park in the field behind us. The old oak tree may have to go."

"Did anyone tell you about Bessie?" You see…. "

"Peggy did. The cow's fine; seems she was allergic to the medication," he said and shook his head. "A guy putting an arm through a window like that was a freakish accident to be sure."

"Think about the window," Elyce had said. I realized then what was wrong with the picture I had envisioned; the shattered glass was on the outside of the barn, indicating that the window had been smashed from within, and not the other way around. In my frenzied state of mind, I had overlooked that important little detail. Shoot, if I had not been zoned out, I'd have known that my ball couldn't have traveled that far.

"It's a relief to know that Jim and Bessie are okay," I said, handing my plate to Dad for a helping of pancakes and bacon. "Does anyone want to see the neat medal I've got?" I took the medal out of my pocket and showed it to mom, who sat next to me.

"It's an unusual medal, Billy; where did you get it?" she asked casually and handed it back to me as though it were a trinket from a Cracker Jacks box.

"I got it from an alien on a space ship," I said, anxious to relate my elaborate tale of suspense and bravery.

"This isn't the time for silly jokes, Billy; put the medal away and eat your breakfast," Dad said.

I could see at a glance that nobody took me seriously. I put the medal in my pocket and reached for the syrup. Yes, indeed, I was home.

Chapter XXVI

EPILOGUE

Seven years have elapsed since that heavenly journey to the stars. For weeks - nay, months - I functioned in the afterglow of the miracle. Elyce and her pink flying machine were double exposed on my every waking hour. Again and again, in memory, I would soar to the hub of the universe; sometimes while in the middle of a conversation with a family member or friend. More than once the trance-like expression on my face alarmed Mom. It was, she said, as though I were somewhere else. Naturally, when asked what was bothering me, I couldn't explain.

When I slept, I dreamed of the enchanting alien. I dreamed of drifting in space and star hopping in spirit, and of other worlds, other realities, and other ethereal beings celebrating the coronation of life on Polduntar in an atmosphere of fire and ice.

Gradually, my obsessive fascination with Elyce subsided along with the compelling awesomeness of the space experience. On the day that I laughed a spontaneous laugh at one of Steve's antics, a beatific calm settled over me and I knew that my mind as well as my body was again earthbound. That night I took the pink medal out of the cricket box, kissed it, and said "Goodbye," to Elyce. Then I put the medal in the back of a drawer in my bureau. My preoccupation with the delightful alien had run its course.

Now when I look back, I realize that the Billy Briarwood who had fled in fright to the summit of Kebor's Mesa one starlit night was not the same Billy Briarwood who had awakened to the call of his name the following morning. The red-haired kid who once sat at an attic window and wondered about the seemingly endless sea of mountains had been transformed by an unbelievable trip to the stars. I know now what is on the other side of the mountains; and on the other side of the Milky Way. I had gained knowledge of the universe I dared not speak of for fear of being committed to an asylum. I was still Billy Briarwood, still fourteen years of age, but mature beyond my years. My courage and strength had been tested in ways others cannot begin to imagine. I see more vividly the things that matter and the things that don't. I no longer question whether or not there is such a thing as divine intervention; I know there is.

Soon after the experience, anxious to photograph the scene of the crash, I gained permission to spend a weekend in the wilderness. On the way there, of course, I stopped at the big red rock formation to check on the shards of white stones only to find that the shards had all mysteriously vanished. Further, there was not a bit of evidence indicating there had been a crash landing on the mountain side.

The revelation overwhelmed me. Had it all been eradicated when Elyce took me backward in time? Backward in time – the phrase slips off the tongue without effort. Albert Einstein explains the phenomenon in his theory of relativity; Elyce demonstrated it in outer space. I had a heap of trouble dealing with it.

If going backward in time eliminated evidence of the crash, then it stands to reason that it also eliminated the crash itself and my space experience as well. But then, what of my memories of it? What of the missing beads and silver coins? And what of the pink medal?

The pink medal is an indisputable tie to Elyce and her pink flying machine. It verifies my sanity and gives credibility to an Odyssey so rare I dare not speak of it. And yet, it happened. It really happened.

Somehow, the idea of my spirit having the capacity to stretch over vast regions of space is not that difficult to comprehend. I know for a fact that a drop of oil placed in a pool of water will diffuse over a large part of the surface.

"Man is fallible," is a phrase that has been bandied around for centuries. Great minds supposedly present unshakable theories one day only to have them debunked the next. Before Columbus proved that the earth is round, men of great intellect held that the sun revolved around the earth and that the earth was flat.

It occurs to me that if man is subject to error, then Polduntarians, too, are subject to error, even if they are on a higher level of existence. In that light, I believe it is possible that Elyce's evaluation of the God-force might be flawed in some ways. Perhaps, she and her people draw conclusions based on their intelligence and the knowledge they have gained, then pursue life toward that end.

I had stood, free of my corporeal self, on the threshold of eternity and witnessed creation taking place right before my eyes; creation Elyce accredited to Aytozee, the most supreme of the supreme. Did that mean the Aytozee force merely belched creative thoughts into a cosmic void and hoped for the best? It may be so, but when you puzzle over the idea long enough it doesn't seem plausible, even for a "primitive" thinker like me. It seems more probable that a force greater than Aytozee exists outside of the whole, draws the blueprints for creation and holds it all – ALL - together.

By Elyce's own admission, Polduntarians are not finely tuned to the ultimate truth. Like mankind, they are seekers still. So, even though they perceive life in the hereafter as a promotion of order, benevolence and contrition, factions may exist which have not yet been revealed, but which may, subsequently, rise to alter their present concept of the matter. Perhaps, as I write, the concept she presented to me no longer holds sway over Polduntarians. With their elevated wisdom and spirituality, maybe that concept has already become a myth, replaced by an updated version of the truth as they now see it; hopefully a version that draws nearer to the absolute.

Nor have I overlooked the possibility that my journey was nothing more than a hypnotic vision induced by the lovely alien. Of course, nothing will convince me of that possibility. Today, I find the mysteries of the universe more intriguing than ever. Since I cannot know the nature of God with absolute certainty, my search will be a never ending saga. Always will I pore over matters yet unknown and, curious, I will seek answers, but I will seek calmly and without undue lust for I know the answers, like flowers, will come in their own time and place.

More than likely, I have come as close to the Supreme Being as I am going to get in my lifetime. I believe a spark of the God force dwells within me, but I am light years away from the God force which, personified as a man, showed the way to eternal happiness - the Christ, who continues to radiate pure love and virtue two thousand years after his death on the cross. I am a mere mortal unequipped to fathom the deepest mysteries of the universe. All I can do is contemplate them and yearn to know the secrets they hold.

If I have learned anything from the space experience and the years I have had to reflect on it, it is the fact that God, or whatever you want to call that unknowable force, is as prevalent in my own backyard as in outer space. Even as stars explode in the great beyond, life goes on in Redbud.

Once David had formulated a plan for his lifelong career he adhered to it. After graduating from high school, he devoted three years working part time for the Pomeroy and Briarwood Construction Company and studying at the Constantine College of Technology. Upon earning a degree in Constructive Engineering, he was awarded a top position in the Pomeroy/Briarwood establishment. He has a solid marriage with Arlene and is currently raising two mischievous rascals; a boy and girl, who I love dearly.

Michael's is another story. After graduating from high school, he became a self-employed Certified Public Accountant. Of course, from the outset, a large portion of his income was derived from the work he did for Dad, Avery, and David.

For several years he seemed perfectly satisfied to live at home within imposed boundaries. Then when he reached the age of twenty-four, he bought the little yellow house below the highway which, after having changed hands a couple of times, had been offered for sale once more. Without a word of explanation, he promptly moved all of his belongings into the little bungalow. Then, pursuant to his move, he and Lena Capelli eloped to Clarksdale and were married by a Justice of the Peace. Lena, who had developed into a sloe-eyed, tawny skinned Latin beauty, had just turned eighteen.

Theirs was not a flash-in-the-pan romance, Michael later informed the family, but a love that had grown from the time Lena was thirteen. For them it had been a matter of waiting patiently for her to become of age.

It was hard to believe that just two weeks prior to the elopement, Lena had stood in cap and gown to receive her diploma and bid farewell to Britt's Bay High School along with me and many of our mutual friends. Now, she was wearing my brother's wedding band and trying to adjust to her in-laws while hastily preparing for a second wedding at Ste. Rita's Roman Catholic Church in Clarksdale to appease her strict Catholic parents. Their love affair would go down in history as one of Redbud's best kept secrets.

In the mean time, I traveled pretty much with the same circle of friends – Steven and Susan Campbell, Ricky Sullivan, Marvin Purcell, Larry Duggan, Cora Cooper, and Lenny and Darlene Schneider. We attended the same functions, shared anecdotes, and laughed a lot harder and longer than necessary to cover our fears of uncertain futures.

In high school, I stubbornly pursued courses that would augment my knowledge of carpentry. Akin to reverse psychology, the fact that Dad had never encouraged me to emulate him, made me all the more determined to do so. Accordingly, each year, my curriculum included such subjects as drafting, woodworking, finishing, layout and design. I became proficient in the use of lathes, sanders, drills, power saws, plumb bobs, levels and planes. I got straight "A's". Alas, it was all for naught; for in truth, the classes gave me no big thrill.

The summer of 1971, at seventeen, I worked for Dad and Avery as a "go-fer" and got a taste of the real deal. In time, I realized that I was martyring myself, struggling to create a relationship with Dad on a level that was not meant to be. Long work hours prevented me from being with Susan as much as I would have liked. I seldom got a chance to play ball with my friends, and side trips into the wilderness were greatly reduced.

In spite of my disillusionment with the field of carpentry, I continued to develop my woodworking skills in my senior year, partly to spare Dad's feelings and partly because I couldn't settle on any specific vocation to undertake in its stead.

With every opportunity, I would strap my knapsack on my back, hang the zoom camera around my neck and hit the trails in the wilderness. If time were short, I'd make Kebor's Mesa my destination; otherwise, I'd strike out for

Mount Angel Head and sometimes venture even further. I had no compunction about staying overnight in a bed of leaves. Wherever I roamed, I attempted to capture nature's rare and beautiful compositions on film. The rewards justified any hardship I endured, and were surpassed only by the pleasure of having been there in the first place. By playing around with the camera and wasting tons of hard-earned money on film, I learned the intricacies of the camera's functions. As a result, I became increasingly adept at the art of photography.

I began to understand the value of light and shadow, how the time of day can change the mood of a subject, and how the most interesting subject is liable to be something easily overlooked. For every dozen or so pictures that ended in the trash can, one had the power to stir my being. In one exceptional scene I captured vapor rising from a watery bog in which a single bright red mushroom boldly saluted the pearly light of dawn.

More with hope than expectation, I took a few of my best shots to Kenaldy University in Willowford to show to Professor Eugene Elrud, who was known as one of the area's most respected authorities in the field of photography. Slight of build and balding, he wore gold-rimmed glasses and, as I would learn, gave one-hundred percent to his students, wanting nothing more than to see them succeed.

When I saw the look of surprised delight spread across his face as he removed "*Mushroom at Daybreak*," from the envelope, I knew that I had found my calling.

He and I talked for hours. I told him of my anxieties and my sensitive position with Dad. He touched on the complexities and varieties of cameras and related equipment; about light sources, exposures, *blocking*, and development. He conveyed to me that being a well-rounded photographer required concentrated study at college level. And, "Yes, a good photographer can make a living at it," he said.

Through Professor Elrud's intervention, and based on my 3.5 grade point average along with the high quality of my pictures, I was awarded a two-year scholarship to Kenaldy upon graduating from high school in June of 1972. To be so honored, gave me the most potent morale booster that I'd had since the mind-blowing encounter with Elyce. Suddenly having a real sense of purpose in life felt extremely good.

That same summer Dad and Avery laid the groundwork for Minnie and Frank Carstaires new home on Packingham Circle away from the bustle of Britt's Bay. The middle aged-couple was responsible for making Dad more elated than I recalled ever seeing him.

He took one of his dream-home designs from the vault at the bank and put it on the table for analysis. Everything that makes a house a home had yet to be incorporated into the simple sketch - blueprints for building construction, electrical circuitry, plumbing, cement work, elevation and so forth. Together, dad, Avery, David and Michael perfected the original concept, modifying and refining where needed.

The plans for the 3,500 square feet of floor space required several months to develop on paper, and another eight months to bring the two-story home to fruition. Precision cut granite had to be ordered for the kitchen and bathroom countertops; marble "lip" molding for the swimming pool and curved, aqua-colored glass for the walls of the three-story, silo-like structure built onto a corner of the house; similar to the one he planned to build into his own home. Someday.

With a backdrop of magnolias, maples, oaks, and evergreens, the inspired dwelling sat high on a hilltop, overlooking a lush rolling countryside. Heralded as a masterpiece, the place became known as the "Carstaires Manor."

College altered relationships. While I pursued a career in photography at Kenaldy University in Plighton, Susan applied her talents at the Concordia College of Fine Arts in Britt's Bay, and Stephen delved into the field of agricultural management at the Freedman College of Agriculture in Willowford. For the first time in our lives the twins and I were deprived of daily contact.

Any reservations I may have had as to the depth of my love for Susan disappeared with the onset of higher learning. I was crazy about her. With four years of college ahead of me, I couldn't afford to become intimately involved; nor could I take Susan for granted. Since neither of us believed in tethering, the most we could promise each other was to hold our racing hormones in check and to wait and see.

A busy schedule and the continual unfolding of unexplored vistas helped. I studied hard and was rewarded in equal measure. Books and a variety of photographic equipment were excellent learning tools, but it was the field trips that intrigued me. The field trips took me into atmospheres and environments distinct from the valley and the world I'd known; the skyscrapers and cosmopolitan flavor of New York City; the colorful, stampeding hordes of people on the streets of New Orleans during Mardi gras; and the endless strands of white-sand beaches bordering the Atlantic Ocean and Gulf of Mexico. How diverse, how phenomenal was my own reality.

In June of 1976, with a Bachelor of Arts degree in Photography and a letter of recommendation from Professor Elrud in my pocket, I kept an appointment with agents of Global Nature Magazine in New York City. After reviewing my credentials and sifting through a raft of photographs I had taken both in conjunction with Kenaldy and on my own in the wilds, they took turns firing questions at me; some related to camera work and others personal. They then extended an offer to me to work as a Junior Photographer with a job description that required my going on various expeditions and performing a multitude of tasks as assigned; whatever that meant. They allotted two months for me to get my affairs in order.

By then, Dad was in the process of putting the finishing touches on his long dreamed-of "Briarwood House," a magnificent creation built snug against Rocky Ridge on the topmost level of his property.

The anticipated date for occupancy coincided almost perfectly with my emergence into the business world. Because I couldn't bear to think of anyone else living in the Hollister House, I arranged to purchase it through Grandpa Hollister. For no matter where in the world I roamed, 117 Nutmeg Lane, in Redbud, North Carolina would always be home to me; that is, if Susan agreed.

Throughout my college years, however few hours I had to spare, I always allotted time for Susan; sometimes inducing her to go into the wilderness with me so that I could fulfill an objective and yet be with her. In my solitude, I invoked images of her; this maiden vessel laden with milk and honey ran round and round the labyrinth of my mind. Now, could I possibly leave Redbud to go to New York without her? The answer was a definite, "No!"

    We had planned a date to go dining and dancing on an evening when I returned from out of town. I decided then to ask her to marry me. I was ready to leave the house when it struck me that I would have to tell her about Elyce before I made my proposal. Hastily, I wrapped the white satin box containing a diamond solitaire ring and the cricket box in the folds of my hiking clothes along with my hiking boots and made a call to Susan.

    "Suz, bring a change of clothes and your hiking boots; I'm on my way," I told her.

    At the Campbell's, I pinned an orchid to the shoulder of her pale yellow ensemble and whisked her off to "The Cliffhanger," the finest eating place in Clarksdale. After surrendering my 1970 Malibu to a valet, I escorted Susan to the fifteenth floor of the Frontenac Building. There, the maitre d' hotel of the dimly-lit supper lounge ushered us to a secluded table for two on a splendid patio overlooking a city defined by millions of dazzling lights. We dined by candlelight, sipped vintage Rhine wine – which we rarely ever did – and danced cheek to cheek to the soft strains of a five-piece band.

Holding her hands across the table, I gazed with frank adoration at her loveliness, noting anew the slight cleft in her chin, her high cheekbones and long-lashed brown eyes. Strands of hair, the color of caramel, escaped from a molded coiffure, making her look pert and pixie-like. It was indeed an evening meant for love and romance - and for divulging deep secrets.

"Do you remember the Day dad took me hunting?" I began.

"Yes, you were very upset afterward," she replied.

"Later that day I got into the last ball game of the season; do you remember that?" I pursued.

"You were the man of the day, Bill, how could I forget."

"Well, I had a strange experience that night, Susan; so strange you may not believe it. I can't talk about it here; we have to go to the summit of Kebor's Mesa."

"Tonight? It's getting late," she protested.

"I need to tell you about Elyce," I blurted. There, I said her name out loud - Elyce - without experiencing any ill effects. The incident further freed me from any emotional ties I may have continued to harbor for the sweet little alien.

"Who is Elyce?" Susan, suddenly interested, wanted to know.

"An alien from outer space," I replied candidly, rising to my feet.

"Bill, are you teasing me?" With creased brow, Susan studied me; her look dubious.

"It's something I have never told anyone, Susan. It's very important to me and not something to be laughed at or taken lightly." The earnestness in my tone must have convinced her.

"Is this why we brought extra clothing? to go to the summit?"

I nodded.

I parked the car at the far end of the Redbud Baseball Field close to the where the old oak tree once grew. Under the fading light of a summer sky, we hurriedly changed out of our finery into climbing clothes. We were able to gain the summit without the use of a flashlight. By the time we reached the pyramidal rock formation the last vestiges of day had fallen below the horizon and the sky was as black as ink. We sat facing the mountains. Memories came flooding back to me.

"There is so much to tell, I don't know where to start," I began, and whipping the cricket box out of my pocket, I opened it to reveal the pink medal. "I don't carry this in my pocket anymore. I brought it with me tonight to show you. A long story accompanies it."

"I want to hear every detail about your experience with Elyce, from beginning to end, Bill."

No other setting could have been more appropriate for the telling of the tale than the star-studded vista before us. The original props were in place, providing visual enhancement for the narration. Susan listened with few interruptions. When I had finished, she fixed her gaze on Mount Angel Head and went inward momentarily, no doubt trying to digest the unexplainable.

"Didn't you say Elyce promised to confirm your story? How is she going to do that?"

I barely heard the question, I was so focused on the stars above, wondering if Elyce, too, remembered our encounter; wondering if she even plied the skyways in her little pink flying machine anymore. Aching to see it once again, I searched the heavens for that bright little object that appeared to be a star running off course. Several times I thought I had spotted it, but I couldn't be sure as my eyes seemed to be playing tricks. Finally, growing weary of the vigil, I put the pink medal back in its container. It was all I had to substantiate my recollections; it told me the journey was real. It was Susan who needed reassurance from Elyce.

Bitterly disappointed, I thought of the engagement ring in my pocket, but didn't have the courage to propose marriage under the circumstances. Turning away from the mountains,

I took a step away from the rim of the mesa, ready to follow the trail back to the valley.

"Bill, Bill, I think I see a shooting star," Susan shouted.

My heart leaped. I spun around and clasped Susan close to my side. Together, wide-eyed, we watched the incredible loops that could have been executed by no other than Elyce in her flying machine. She hurtled straight down toward the earth, sheered away at the last second and began to describe broad concentric circles that spiraled ever higher in the sky.

Her ship had become but a fly-speck when Susan and I, in unison, waved "Goodbye." I should never have underestimated the prowess of the alien. The ship immediately shot back to earth, hovered directly in front of us, wobbled in a salute - and disappeared.

Without saying a word, we continued to sit trance-like and mull over the unbelievable scene we had just witnessed until the tower clock pealed the hour of eleven, and then we both wanted to speak at once.

"Do your still love Elyce?" Susan asked.

The Riddle of Kebor's Mesa

"Now do you believe me?" I asked.

That brought us back to earth. We laughed and held each other tight.

"I would have believed you regardless, Bill. But gosh…. actually becoming a part of your story has me in a daze. Gosh," she said again and shuddered. "What are the chances of this happening? Once in a thousand years?"

"Once in a hundred thousand years maybe; maybe the chances are even rarer than that," I replied.

"I'm so deeply touched I won't be the same for weeks – no, months."

I tucked a finger under her chin and forced her to face me. "As for Elyce, I'll always love her; however, it's not a romantic kind of love, but the love for a being that transcends worldliness; a holy spirit you worship from afar. It was extremely important to me that she appear to confirm my story to you. I'll be forever grateful to her for that."

I took a deep breath and surged on. "You, Susan, are my earth angel. I need you with both feet on the ground." I went on to explain the situation with Global Nature Magazine and the short time I had before I would be traveling to alternate locations for filming. I mentioned my sentimental feelings about the Hollister House and asked if she would consider it a place to always come back to. "We can always rent it out if we are going to be gone for any length of time."

"I get a strong feeling that you are trying to tell me something, Bill; what is it?"

"Only that I'm madly in love with you; that I want you to go with me as my wife when I go to New York. Say you will marry me, Susan," I said, and showed her the diamond solitaire in the white satin box. "This belonged to Grandma Sarah; Grandpa gave it to me to give to you."

The sight of the diamond made her gasp. She turned her eyes from the precious gem to the sky above and back again. "'Yes,' would have been my answer if you had presented me with a chip of glass from a pop bottle, Bill. This is exquisite and I will cherish it always, but mostly for its sentimental value," she said, her limpid pools brimming over and staining her cheeks with tears of happiness. "Because it came from you and your grandmother, and because it reminds me of Elyce's star ship, it is irreplaceable. I have always loved you Bill; always; since the time we shared play pens. Will you place the ring on my finger?"

I slipped the ring on her finger and kissed her hungrily again and again; her warm soft lips meeting mine with the same intense ardor.

We were Adam and Eve in our own little paradise caught up in a moment of pure bliss. Driven by a burning desire to consummate our love, I crushed her to me, wanting to hold her forever, to consume her, to mold her flesh to mine. Her sensitive nipples, on breasts as hard as crisp red apples, peaked at my touch, further inflaming me.

"Susan, Susan, how much longer must I wait?" I whispered.

In answer, she began to fumble with the buttons on my shirt. The next thing we knew we were tearing articles of clothing from each other and tossing them on the ground. High on the summit of Kebor's Mesa I drew her nude body to mine and gave in to a surge of passion gone out of control. Still, I had the presence of mind to ask before I entered her, "Susan, are you sure you're ready for this?"

"Yes, Bill," she answered huskily, "as sure as God works miracles.

"

THE END